The Spirit of the North Wind

THE Spirit OF THE North Wind

ANTHONY ANSELMO

Black Bears & Blueberries Publishing

The Spirit of the North Wind
Copyright © 2023 by Anthony Anselmo

All rights reserved. No part of this publication may be reproduced, stored in a retrieval system, or transmitted in any form or by any means without the prior written permission of the publisher, except in brief quotations embodied in critical articles and reviews.

This is a work of fiction. All characters, organizations, and events portrayed in this novel are either products of the author's imagination or are used fictitiously.

ISBN 979-8-9862981-3-9

Cover illustration and book design by Paul Nylander | Illustrada

Published by Black Bears & Blueberries Publishing, Duluth, Minnesota
www.BlackBearsAndBlueberries.com
A Native owned non-profit publishing company, with a focus on creating and developing Native children's books for all young people written by Native writers and illustrated by Native artists.

*This book is dedicated to all those
who battle their very own ghosts,
may you always stay one step ahead.*

CHAPTER 1

Leaving Town

Thirteen-year-old Sody Fairbanks plodded down the shoulder of main street carrying a crumpled five-dollar bill his mother had given him for ice cream. It was early in the afternoon, but an impending thunderstorm shut out much of the remaining light from the sun. As darkness slowly blanketed the town, Sody quickened his pace. His sneakers were worn to shambles from last summer's escapades. A crumbling pair of flat-bottomed shoes that had seen their fair share of skateboarding and hot summer days playing basketball with his buddy Dakota at the old park in town.

The summer's first thunderstorm brought a dark, ominous presence to a previously bluebird day. It swept in from the west, building up speed and power across the vast plains of the Dakotas before looming over the humble town of Togo, Minnesota. The town's lone gas station sat at the intersection across from a small café. Its awning lights flickered on and off, on and off, like something out of a horror movie.

Sody felt raindrops on his bare arms and peered up to see the clouds start to spiral in odd formations. Every leaf from the tall willow trees that lined the street swirled wildly. He dashed to the corner cafe and threw the door open. The bells on the handle clanged, signifying his arrival. The lights from the blue and red neon OPEN sign in the window flickered lazily.

"You runnin' from something dear?" asked the lone cashier with eyeballs nearly popping out of her head.

Sody motioned to the window. "It's about to storm, can't you see?"

Down the street a wall of rain swept angrily towards the café.

The bells on the door clanged again, and another customer arrived and shuffled to a seat at the counter. The man stood abnormally tall and gaunt like a ghost. He hobbled on a cane and was covered by a much too large black coat that appeared to float on his skeletal frame. An oversized hood masked most of the face. Sody immediately started to sweat. It was about to storm indeed.

"Sure looks that way, Sody," said the cashier while eyeing the new customer. "I thought you guys were moving today."

"Huh?" he stammered. "Oh, right, no . . . we leave tomorrow." Looking down at the floor he shuffled his feet.

"I don't want to go. All my friends are here, and I'll never get to taste one of your famous malts ever again."

The cashier, sporting an oversized name tag on her gray blouse that read *Sandy*, frowned. "Tell ya what, you can get whatever you want today. On the house." Sandy had sandy blonde hair. Ironic! And it bobbed on her head every time she moved. She also perpetually chewed spearmint gum. Sody could tell it was spearmint because she always chewed it with her mouth open and he could see the bright green color of the gum.

"On the house?"

Chuckling, Sandy managed to respond, "It means I won't charge ya nothin."

"Oh, Okay!" Sody let slip his first grin in a long time, "Thanks! In that case, I'll take a large chocolate malt."

"You sure? That's what you always get. I have been known to make a pretty mean chocolate fudge sundae too."

He quietly perused the large white board hanging on the wall above the ice creams. Orange, blue, and green dry erase marker displayed myriads of options he never even thought of trying: peppermint bon bon, moose tracks, rocky road, chocolate chip cookie dough and even birthday cake ice cream.

"Yeahh," he finally said with a thick Minnesotan accent, "I think I'll still take a malt." He grinned, and Sandy winked at him before going to work on his order. They both kept one eye on the stranger sitting at the far end of the counter. The man stared straight ahead, making no such acknowledgment that anyone else existed. The hair pricked up on Sody's back. He had never seen this person before. And in a small town like Togo, everybody knows everybody.

"Earth to Sody." He snapped out of his trance as Sandy's words seemed to come from a dream. "Thought I lost you there for a second. Here is your malt. Now get home safely and tell your folks I said hi." Sandy handed him the large Styrofoam cup of chocolatey wonder and shooed him out the door.

Walking home he felt a little bit lighter. He even skipped a hop or two before a crash of thunder shook him to the bone. The earth shuddered as the thunder boom seemingly rumbled the entire county. Rain slashed down from the skies in sheets, immediately saturating the lawns and forming small rivers along the sides of the streets. Everything was wet. Wet and dark.

Sody sloshed into his house—a home that would be his for only one more night. His parents thought the ice cream would perhaps lighten the dread of moving away from the house he and his siblings grew up in, but the storm reversed that effect.

"Why are your clothes so wet?" Sody's older sister, Jamie, sneered as soon as he walked through the door.

"Because it's raining outside, duh," he mumbled back while peeking down at his now watery chocolate malt and the small puddle of water on the floor from his sopping wet clothes.

He shrugged and tossed the remainder of the malt into the garbage in the kitchen. It was their last night in town, and it was already as miserable as he imagined. The family photos had all been taken down from the walls and packed neatly away. The only sign of their existence was the faded colors left on the wall where the hanging memories once greeted the house's many visitors.

The Fairbanks family frequently had visitors at their modest, forest green house that lined the main street of Togo. A couple of the neighborhood kids often stopped by on their way to the park to beg Sody's parents, Shelly and Dario, if the kids could go play basketball or watch the adults play softball at the old Togo school on Tuesday nights.

Drew, his older brother, enjoyed more freedom than the rest. He and his cronies spent most of their summers hanging out at the park, skateboarding around the rundown tennis court wearing their cut-off shirts and flat bottom sneakers. Sody grew jealous of this, so he resorted to shooting hoops in his driveway on the basketball hoop hanging above the garage door. His dad had painted the backboard a bold blue and yellow—the school colors, but he neglected to make sure the rim was ten feet from the ground. Sody knew that was the standard height, but was equally certain this hoop hung about six inches too low.

"Good enough for the girls we go with," his dad had said after installing it. Whatever that meant.

There were countless summers of this. Summers of filthy hands from playing basketball in a dirt driveway pocked with potholes filled to the brim with rainwater and mud. Summers of bare feet and bee stings. Of bike rides and skateboarding. Of chocolate malts and Jones soda, which were the very taste of summer itself. Of freedom personified.

Summer was a time Sody always looked forward to. It was a time all boys his age lived for. Where the soles of sneakers were worn down to nothing and the burden of homework and tests long forgotten. The very thought of school tucked away into the corners of the attic like an old book to collect dust. But not this summer. This summer he'd be dragged away from his friends to move away from his childhood home and move into a camper trailer while the family's new house was built.

"Mom, I don't want to leave. I won't get to see my friends all summer." Sody complained, pacing around the nearly empty living room while juggling a football and basketball.

"You'll get to see them, hun. Don't you worry." His mom sat cross-legged on the living room carpet and peered up from a box she was swiftly shoving books into. "We're not moving to a different country, you know. The new place is only a half hour away. Right next to grandpa and grandma's."

"Well. . ." Sody contemplated. "I guess that's not *so* bad. But still, I like it here. Togo is special. It's home." He slumped down onto the couch and kicked his feet up. His mom stared at the perpetually dirty socks on her son's feet. She could not seem to come to terms with how they were *always* dirty and *always* full of holes.

Another loud bang from the thunder shook the house. The family's chocolate lab, Mocha, quivered with fear at the deafening noise. She sauntered over and took a seat next to Sody's feet. She dreaded storms as much as the kids dreaded leaving their hometown. Mocha rested her head on Sody's knee as if to say, "pet me, I'm scared" or maybe she was saying, "it's okay, I'm here for you." Mocha was a good family dog, and she would prove to be so much more than just a pet in the coming weeks.

Shelly sat in the living room with her four kids where only a dark green couch and TV stand remained. The ceiling-high chestnut wardrobe and all of its mysterious contents no longer loomed in the back corner of the room. Sody always thought the wardrobe might lead to Narnia, but never checked for fear of something else possibly lurking inside. The piano that his sister Jamie used to play was also missing. Sody would miss smashing the keys in an attempt to make his own music. Even his mom's enormous plants, which looked more like small trees, were gone. It was all gone. Packed away and waiting.

Lightning struck somewhere west of town, but it would start no fires tonight. The rain was coming down far too hard for that, so hard in fact, it sounded like a million tennis balls dribbling on the roof of the house.

"Kids! Kids, come downstairs!" yelled a voice from somewhere deep down in the basement.

One by one they all got up grumbling and shuffled down the hardwood stairs in a mini procession before flinging open the saloon doors that lead to the basement family room. Their dad sat atop one of the three wooden barstools, waiting for them with a great big grin on his face. The stool squeaked loudly as Dario swiveled on it.

"Why are you so happy, Dad?" cried Jamie.

"Shhh . . . listen," he replied, his grin stretching from ear to ear.

He walked over to the corner where the ancient stereo sat on a dusty wooden shelf and turned the volume knob up. It didn't take long before everybody grinned. The speakers blared *American Pie* by Don McLean—one of the Fairbanks family's favorite songs. A large weight lifted and dissolved out of the room sometime during the growing build-up of the song. Sody, Drew, and the youngest Fairbanks sibling, Keegan, all stood up on the faded green, L-shaped couch dancing to the beat while their sister Jamie held the TV remote like a microphone and belted out, "Drove my Chevy to the levee, but the levee was dry!"

Their parents watched and laughed and sighed as the kids got lost in the song. The music died later that day, but a new tune was on the horizon.

CHAPTER 2

The Escape

Sody knew how awfully short and skinny and undersized he was for his age, but it never appeared to bother him. What he lacked in size, he made up for in heart. When he wanted something, he usually got it, no matter the obstacles or the stern objections from his parents. His unflinching stubbornness to do what he wanted blessed him *and* cursed him. Not only this, but Sody had a bucket of luck tucked away somewhere deep inside his being.

A deeply tanned skin accentuated a hawk-beaked nose that extended out from his high cheekbones. His Ojibwe blood, long since removed from its native grounds and running thin like a trickling stream in late summer, still showed through. He always had his black hair cut short in a crew style, especially in the summer because he believed it made him lighter and faster and more aerodynamic. He tried anything that might make him just a little bit faster and jump a little bit higher.

Some days he aspired to be Tony Hawk and other days he wanted to be Lamar Jackson or Travis Pastrana or like his big brother, Drew. Sody worshiped his older brother, like many younger brothers do. But Drew differed from Sody in many ways. Drew was a rabble-rouser. A rebellious sixteen-year-old with shaggy black hair, who loved to skateboard and took great pleasure in breaking the rules. In a way, the two brothers were complete opposites. Sody *almost* always followed the rules and rarely got into trouble. Perhaps because he studied Drew's mistakes and learned how to be craftier and avoid getting caught. Sody appeared to be a model kid to most outsiders, but he had a curious, if not mischievous side to him he kept well hidden.

In the weeks leading up to the big move away from Togo, Sody plotted a master escape. With school still in session, he made plans with his best friends, Chester and Dakota, who lived close to town. The plan consisted of him staying with them this summer and his parents could do nothing about it. If his parents wanted him to move, they were in for a dogfight, and Sody could be a pitbull.

"Alright, so this is what we need to do." Sody drew in the sand on the playground with his pointer finger. His two best friends sat cross-legged in front of him. "On move out day I'm going to get on my bike and ride out of town to your house, Chester. I'll make sure my parents are busy packing, so they don't see me leave." He peered up from his drawing with a look of utter seriousness. "Chester, you tell your mom that my parents had to delay the move and that I'm only staying a few days."

Chester carefully pondered this for a moment with his chubby hand on his chin. "Okay, that seems believable. I don't think she'll care," he finally retorted. "She likes when you come over anyways because 'it gets my brother and me out of the house."" He finished while mocking his mom's voice, throwing up air quotations and rolling his eyes. The three boys burst out laughing and rolled over on the ground.

"Wait, but where do I come in?" Dakota chimed in after the three finally quit laughing.

"I was getting to that. After I stay a few days at Chester's, his mom is going to start asking when my family is moving. When she starts getting curious, I'll tell her I'm leaving in a day or two." Sody smirked mischievously. "So when I have to leave, instead of going home I'll leave from Chester's and just bike to your house and we'll tell your parents the same thing."

"That's genius," said Dakota.

"I'd say," added Chester. "But there's just one thing . . . Won't your parents come looking for you? I mean, they're going to notice that you are gone, won't they?"

Sody appeared stumped. "That's a good point, Chester. You've always been the brains of this group. I'll think on it. In the meantime, you should think about it too and let me know if you have any big ideas."

"Deal."

"Done deal. Secret shake on it so nobody backs out." Sody stared at them with a serious look in his eye. The boys shook hands. They had a deal.

Chester Heartsfield and Sody Fairbanks were nearly the same age, but that is where their shared physical traits stopped. Sody was an Ojibwe and Chester was white with bleach blonde hair and piercing blue eyes that told no lies and had a body built like a steer. His loyalty to his friends never wavered and the three boys had become best friends when they first met at Sody's mom's daycare when they were only four years old. Dakota Lindgren happened to be a grade below the other two but carried many similarities with Sody. They looked so alike, in fact, they were often mistaken as brothers to those who didn't know them. Sody, Chester and Dakota felt like they *were* brothers.

While most of the Fairbanks clan intended to move out of their house today, Sody was ready to put his plan to stay in Togo for one final summer into play. The birds outside the upstairs window awakened with the rising of the sun, singing their morning hymn to the world. Even the squirrels were out chattering earlier than usual. The animals were cheering him on. They didn't want him to leave either. They knew how much he admired them.

Sody slowly rolled out of bed and shucked the sleep from his eyes. Standing near the edge of his ancient twin bed he peered around the room and for the first time he realized how sad he truly felt to be leaving his home. Not a single Lego lay strewn about the floor waiting to be stepped on, or fortified Lincoln log cabins armed with toy soldiers. These, along with his matchbox cars, had been tossed in a moving box days ago marked *toys*. The only signs remaining that someone lived on the second floor was the silly putty Keegan had left open and forgotten underneath his bed that left a large, pink splotch stuck in the navy-blue carpet and the gigantic T-Rex Sody drew on the wall with a magic marker at age three. Maybe he could have gotten away with blaming Drew or Jamie for the mural, but he was the only sibling obsessed with dinosaurs, not to mention he signed his name directly beneath the T-Rex.

His mom had to admit it was pretty impressive her three-year-old could craft something that good and spell his name right at such a young age, even if his "y" was backwards. But this didn't make her any less angry when she first discovered it on the wall.

Downstairs, Sody's dad sang cheerfully. *Too cheerfully*, Sody thought.

> *Morning has broken, like the first morrrning,*
> *Blackbird has spoken, like the first birrrd.*

His dad's favorite song by Cat Stevens. Perhaps more so than the hymn, he loved waking the kids up with his own singing because it always worked, and they always jarred him about it. He took great delight in teasing them, especially in the mornings when they clung to sleep and had little tolerance.

Only in his mid-thirties, his dad's hair had slowly started to go grey from teaching the 6th graders at the Togo Middle School and coaching the JV basketball team in the winter. He liked to keep a full schedule, and the kids made him feel young and old all at the same time. He enjoyed teaching and coaching them though. If he could inspire a few, he was content. Perhaps the grey came from trial and error as he tried to find the best way to empower the youth.

In the kitchen, he poured pancake batter onto the griddle and started crisping bacon in a cast iron on the stovetop. The fragrance of breakfast sifted through the house, eventually reaching Sody, Keegan and Drew, who finally stirred from their beds upstairs. Jamie had been up for an hour already and stood in the kitchen helping her dad with the pancakes when their mom peeked in to eye the bacon, making sure her husband didn't cook it to a crisp again.

The kitchen was quite quaint, its floor made up of white and baby blue faux tile with matching blue cabinets. From the small window above the metal sink, one could view the backyard where the large dog kennel stood, and the small swing set and sandbox sat eerily empty. A haven where the kids used to reign for days on end. A haven that would soon belong to another family. As Dario peered out the window, he became troubled by the thought of anyone else but his family enjoying that special backyard. The memories of watching them grow up sent shivers up his spine and pricked the hairs up on his neck. The sound of padded feet brought him back to reality.

"Good morning Sody, you look awfully spry for someone who just woke up," said his dad. "You haven't forgotten we are moving today, have you?" He sized up Sody, who had raced into the kitchen and poked his sister while she flipped the cakes.

"Of course, I remembered. But you always say to stay positive, even when we are down."

"Wow, you're actually taking some of my advice. You're smarter than you look," said his dad as he tousled his son's hair.

Sody's positivity stemmed from his escape plan that he assumed would run its course rather smoothly. He would not be moving today, not if he could help it. With the plan already agreed upon, all he had to do was execute it.

"Not again Dario, look at this bacon!" cried Shelly.

The bacon had blackened to a crisp and the pan smoked hotly.

Dario shrugged his shoulders. "Sorry dear. Sody here was distracting me," he said, winking at his son.

"It's true, it's my fault mom."

"Well, oh well. . ." his mom sighed, hands on hips. "At least we have some more in the fridge." She patted around the barren fridge searching for the rest of the bacon. "Where is it?"

"That's all of it," replied his dad, pointing at the stove, clenching and baring his teeth to brace from his wife's scolding.

His mom simply shook her head and slipped away to the bedroom to finish packing the rest of her belongings. She honestly wasn't much of a fan of eating the delicious underside of a pig anyways.

Keegan and Drew sat quietly on the living room couch. Keegan started to get up to turn on the television for the morning cartoons, but quickly realized the TV was no longer there. Just an empty cherrywood entertainment stand looking out of place in the vacant room. The TV had been packed away, awaiting its journey to the new home. Instead, they gazed out the picture window at the front yard where Mocha trotted around, roaming her territory one last time.

With the house buzzing with his siblings and parents moving boxes and clothes out of their rooms, Sody finally saw his chance to get away. His mom and dad were busy barking orders to "bring this outside" and "no, don't put that there." While they were all inside, he took out a box of kitchenware. Once outside, he dashed to the trailer sitting in the driveway and ripped his bike from it.

It was no ordinary bike, but a new Huffy BMX bike he received as a birthday present from his parents back in the spring.

A beautiful deep black and orange paint job made it stick out like a Ferrari in farm country. It was easily the fastest bike in town. It boasted rear pegs that his brother Keegan stood on while Sody rode up and down the streets of Togo. The bike was nearly mint, almost pristine, except for the small chunk of the seat that had been snarled off by the neighbor's obese and voraciously hungry pug, Pugsley. Pugsley had eyes like black golf balls and jowls like Jabba the Hutt that were perpetually covered in slobber. The beast had dutifully earned the nickname "The Cow". Partly because he was quite plump and partly because everyone in town was convinced the dog had four stomachs. Something so small should not be able to eat so much.

Chewed up seat and all, Sody flew down the short driveway and onto the street heading east, skidding his tires in the loose dirt on his way to Chester's. Pugsley started to run after him, but quickly lost his breath and waddled gingerly back home to squeeze into his almost too tiny doghouse. Sody's heart pounded. *Did they see me?* He wondered. Part of him hoped they had so that they might catch him before he left town. But he dared not look back now, he'd made up his mind to get away. Stubbornly, he tucked away the thought of what his parents would feel when they realized he was missing and pedaled on.

On his way to Chester's, armed with only his backpack and bike, he passed the park where he spent hours upon hours with his friend Dakota shooting baskets on the basketball hoop with the old chain net. The park where he and his sister Jamie used to see who could swing the highest and jump out the farthest. Where he felt like a pro skateboarder when his brother Drew let him hang out with his friends and skate on the unforgiving ramps they built out of spare wood and nails. The place where he learned cuss words from the letters etched in the wood of the top platform on the playground. The park where summer was and maybe always would be.

At the sudden recollection of all these thoughts and memories, Sody began to cry. Tears streamed down his face and dropped silently to the road beneath. His vision, partially blurred, flooded with memories and fear of the future, but he pedaled on. He had to. He needed one more summer in Togo.

It took the rest of the Fairbanks family a while before realizing Sody was gone. His parents assumed he just disappeared for a little while, which he always seemed to do when work needed to be done.

"Have you seen your brother?" Shelly asked Jamie.

"No, I bet he's back at the fort. Or on top of the dog kennel."

"The dog kennel?"

"Yes, the dog kennel." Jaime sounded slightly annoyed that her mom was unaware of this. "He sometimes goes up there when we are playing hide and seek."

The kennel had a makeshift roof over the top which Dario built with long pieces of tin laid across the chain link fence. The low hanging branches from the towering spruce trees that surrounded the kennel, crowded the makeshift roof. It formed a natural fort, and a likely spot for Sody to be hiding.

"Sody! Sody, come help finish up, we gotta go!" yelled his dad.

No response.

"Sody! We'll leave you here if you don't come back!" An empty promise he knew, but it was worth a shot.

Still no response.

The rest of the Fairbanks stopped their packing to search for their runaway rogue. But by the time Sody's family noticed his disappearance, he had already turned off the highway and onto the dirt road leading to Chester's. With only two more miles to go he started to feel a little less anxious about being found out and a little more excited to have unshackled himself from the certain misery of moving.

He raced on despite the muddiness of the dirt road. Yesterday's storm had punished the gravel and created a muddy, sludgy mess that was a job to pedal through. His shoes and pant legs quickly became sodden with the mud splashing up from his tires. Looking down, he noticed one of his shoes was untied and the laces about to slide between the gear and the chain of the bike. He quickly tapped his brakes, but in the hurry to stop he accidentally squeezed his front brake too hard, causing the bike to pivot on the front wheel and launch him like a space shuttle through the air.

Commencing countdown, engines on!

After what seemed like forever soaring through the air, he finally landed in a large mud puddle alongside the road.

Splash!

Sody lifted his head up from the puddle and looked back to see his bike turned upside down in the road. His backpack was the only piece of him that wasn't completely drenched. Still laying on his stomach in the puddle he let out a raucous laugh, imagining he must look like a lost turtle on the side of the road. The laugh brought pain as well, and he soon realized his ribs were aching and his hands and arms full of cuts and scrapes from the coarse dirt.

"Why couldn't I have landed in the grass at least," he grunted out loud to no one.

Finally, he pulled himself from the mucky road to investigate the scrapes and cuts on his arms. After retying his shoe, he clambered back onto his upturned bike and continued his trek, unaware of the fear his family was currently experiencing because they couldn't find him.

Sody spotted something streaking around the corner in the road ahead. Chester.

"What *happened* to you?" Chester exclaimed.

"Shoe came untied. I slammed on my brakes before it got caught in the chain, but apparently, I hit the wrong brakes. I still haven't figured out this new bike."

"You're soaked!" Chester was laughing now.

"Yeah, yeaaah I know. Keep laughing, but when you fall into a puddle don't be asking me for any help 'cause I'll just sit there and laugh at you."

"Okay, okay I'm sorry," he admitted, kicking up his bike's kickstand. "Let's head back to my place, my mom's making brownies."

The thought of this made Sody's mouth water. Chester's mom made the world's best brownies and he had forgotten to grab lunch before he exiled himself from the move. The two trudged on through the mud and the sludge still lingering on County Road 229. A road well-traveled by Sody and Chester over the years. A road with countless memories still clinging to the tracks in the dirt left by their bike tires.

While Sody pulled up to his friend's driveway, back in town his family became more and more desperate in their search. They tried the corner café, the gas station, even the park. No one had seen him anywhere. This didn't come as a huge surprise as a town of one hundred people didn't have a lot of witnesses.

The Fairbanks piled themselves into their silver Suburban, which was already packed to the ceiling with boxes and clothes and drove frantically around town searching for any sign of their kin.

"Sody! Sody, where are you!?" his mom hollered out the car window.

"What are you guys going to do to him once we find him?" Jamie questioned her parents with a hint of curiosity.

"Just hush right now. We'll worry about that later. Are you guys sure he didn't say anything about where he was going?" their mom responded with desperation in her voice.

"No, he never said anything. I saw that his bike was gone though. It wasn't on the trailer." There was a silence that echoed through the vehicle after Jamie said this.

"Chester's," both parents said in unison. "Why didn't you say something sooner?"

"I didn't think it was important."

In the summer before, when Sody was only twelve, his parents had reluctantly let him and Jamie bike to Chester's. Chester's older brother, Mitchell, was in the same grade as Jamie and the four of them spent many summers together. Mitch and Chester's mom, Franny, had the great idea. Shelly finally agreed to let them all bike to Franny's as long as Franny would drive behind them and make sure nothing bad happened. Ever since that day, Sody biked over to their house any chance he got and vice versa.

"Well hey Sody, did you swim here?" Franny exclaimed after Sody plodded through the front door of her log home. "Here let me grab you a towel."

Sody answered through chattering teeth, "Th-thanks Franny, I was starting to get a little cold."

"Oh, I know, I could hear your teeth chattering as soon as you boys started down the driveway." She tossed Sody a large towel displaying a Pokéball and Pikachu.

Franny was like a second mom to Sody. He spent so much time at their place it became his home away from home. The green roofed log house sat on the edge of a small field bordered by mysterious woods that stretched for miles in either direction. A long dirt driveway led up to the front door and was annually fringed with little puddles this time of year, which were home to loads of leopard frogs the kids loved to chase after and catch. A trampoline stood alone in the front yard, standing the tests of time with the blue protective mat missing for as long as anyone could remember.

Sody clopped up the stairs to change into dry clothes, each step on the hardwood stairs creaking as he clambered to the second floor. As he stepped into the perpetually messy room that Chester and Mitchell shared, he couldn't help but smile. *Just as every boy's room should be*, he thought to himself. After changing, he raced downstairs to meet Chester. They both grabbed a brownie from the pan sitting on the stove and marched out the door to see what the day had yet to offer.

"What should we do?" asked Chester.

"Oh no." Sody turned as pale as a ghost.

Chester caught Sody's stare and turned to see a silver Suburban rumbling down the driveway.

"Quick, follow me!" he shouted.

The two boys took off behind an old, gutted, white house that still stood next to the newly built log home. The house was in the process of being torn down. Chester grabbed a tall silver extension ladder laying on the ground and hoisted it up. The top just barely reached the edge of the roof.

"You first, Sody."

"Okay, hold the ladder and pray for me. If the fall doesn't kill me, my parents probably will!"

Sody's tiny frame raced up the ladder. Once at the top, he turned around and laid on the edge of the roof to hold the top of the ladder while his partner in crime clambered up to join him. Just as Chester reached the top, they could hear the crunch of rocks crushing underneath the tires of the Suburban before it came to a stop.

"Shhh . . . follow me." Chester whispered as he duck-walked to the other end of the house where the old house's leaning chimney stood.

The two boys slunk their way to the chimney. They heard the doors of the Suburban slam shut. A moment later there came a low creaking sound as Chester's mom opened up the screen door on the main house.

"I'm dead. I'm so dead Chester. How did they know I was here?"

"I have no idea. Maybe Jamie told on you."

"She couldn't have known though. I tell her just about everything, but I never told her about our plan."

"Well, it doesn't matter how they found out. What matters right now is hiding." Chester sounded like an army general. Confident and decisive. "They're gonna have to force us down from here. I don't want you to move away."

"Okay, let's do it. I don't want to move either. It's not fair they're making me leave." Sody sounded fearful.

The screen door creaked again. Sody and Chester froze, crouched behind the red brick chimney like hostages. If there was one thing they were good at, it was hiding. They had years of experience running and hiding from their siblings and parents.

All the shingles had since been removed from the roof, some of them by Sody and Chester and Mitchell in the weeks previous, and the strength of the sun heated up the tar paper so hot it felt like lava on their feet.

"I can't stay here much longer Chester. This roof is so hot. Are they still down there?" whispered Sody.

Chester peeped his head out from behind the chimney searching for any sign of their parents.

"Sody . . . Chester! You guys come back, Sody has to go." yelled Chester's mom with an air of sadness, half hoping the boys were out of earshot.

Her two sons had become great friends with Sody over the past nine years and it broke her heart to see him and Jamie and the rest of the Fairbanks clan leaving town.

"We better go Chester . . . I don't want you to get in trouble too," stammered Sody.

"Yeah, I guess we should."

"I might be leaving town, but we are still going to be best friends. Let's make a pact right here, up on this roof, to be best friends forever."

"Best friends forever," replied Chester with such sincerity Sody knew nothing could ever change their friendship.

The two boys slowly slunk out of the protection of the chimney. Walking towards a new and unknown future. Could they really still be friends living thirty miles apart? They would probably never see each other except in school. This was something thirteen-year-old boys worried about.

Sody felt the glare from his parents penetrating his impregnable pride as he lowered himself off the ladder. He felt like a dog with his tail between his legs.

"Sorry I lied to you, Franny." Sody said to Chester's mom, "I just didn't want to ever leave. It's so much fun here."

"It's okay, Sody. We don't want you guys to leave either. You can still come over whenever you want, you'll just have to have your mom bring you instead of biking over here. Thirty miles is a long way to bike." she said and winked at Sody.

Sody hugged Chester and Franny goodbye and dragged himself into the Suburban. They weren't half-way down the driveway before his parents turned around in the car.

"What were you thinking? We were worried sick!" his mom cried out.

"We're just glad you are safe, Sody. You really had everyone scared." His dad acted a shade calmer. "We thought you had been kidnapped."

It was like good cop, bad cop.

"I'm sorry. I wasn't thinking. I guess I never thought about how you guys would feel if I ran away."

"Sody, you can't just run away from your problems. Life is going to knock you down sometimes. It's not always going to be an easy ride, and this wasn't an easy decision for your mom and me to make. I know you might not think so, but it's true. Sometimes you are going to have to face your fears and trust everything will be okay," said his dad sternly, yet sincerely.

Sody nodded his head as he thought about what his dad just said. He was always right it seemed, even when he didn't want him to be. Dario resembled his father, Sody's grandpa, George. They looked at hard times and change as something to grow from and something that you can't always control. Sody struggled with this. He knew getting upset or scared over these things was trivial, but boy was life difficult sometimes!

The silver Suburban lumbered on down County Road 229 hauling a towering trailer and the Fairbanks who set off to their new home, one with unpredictable adventures and unforeseeable lessons.

CHAPTER 3
Lake Napoleon

The lake sparkled silently with waters calm and pristine. Shallow, underwater springs fed the lake and made the water nearly crystal clear. The sun had started its ascent, rising above the trees, leaving a blinding glare that reflected off the surface of Lake Napoleon. Although it was only ten o'clock in the morning on the first week of June, a muggy heat wave began to settle over northern Minnesota. It was just the start of a long, hot summer.

In a small lot, nestled on the backdrop of a poplar grove, sat the Fairbanks's old camper trailer. Its windows looked out at the lake, keeping an eye on the weather and the height of the sun. The camper stood thirty-two feet long and leaned low to one side. Although seemingly large for a camper, when inhabited by six people, it made for an awfully tight fit. Something the Fairbanks family soon found out. On the back corner of the lot stood an old red, scraggy shed that housed the family's fishing rods, tackle boxes, and a two-wheeled weed trimmer. It was also packed to the ceiling with swim noodles and inner tubes, making it nearly impossible for anyone to enter.

Outside a loud, persistent buzzing penetrated the thick air. *Cicadas?* Sody thought to himself. *In June?* The sound grew with the rising of the sun and the heat of the day until it seemed that the humidity itself created the noise. What little breeze the day puffed out limited any escape from the blanketing warmth of an early summer.

Keegan blitzed out of the camper and bee-lined towards the lake, followed in close pursuit by Jamie. Sody stopped gazing up at the giant red pines around the fire pit and chased after.

"Last one in is a rotten egg!" yelled Keegan into the air.

Splash!

He was already in the lake. Soon after, Sody sprinted along the dock, passing his sister, and jumped as far out as he could, landing right next to his younger brother.

Splash!

They both turned to watch Jamie, the rotten egg, plug her nose and leap off the dock.

Splash!

"You're a rotten egggg!" exclaimed both brothers in unison.

"You guys always cheat! It's not fair."

"Maybe you should be faster." Keegan answered before diving under the surface of the cool water.

All three started splashing each other, laughing and shouting and relieved to have liberated themselves from the sweltering sun.

Meanwhile, their oldest sibling, Drew, was still sleeping on the overly stiff, salmon pink fold-out couch in the camper. Drew could sleep through an air raid and usually remained conked out until noon during the summer. Their mom skinnied up so she could sneak past the couch on her way back to the tiny kitchen. She was making potato salad and cutting up a watermelon for an afternoon snack for the kids. Dressed in white shorts and a lime green tank-top with the air conditioning unit on full blast, she could find no escape from the gripping heat of the Minnesota summer.

She was a petite woman, with reddish-brown hair that bobbed off her shoulders as she walked. She constantly buzzed around like a bee, busy cooking or cleaning or both. She loved cooking, or at least she made it seem like it. She could make a liverwurst taste like a New York Strip. The Fairbanks family knew they were extremely spoiled by her culinary skills.

"Drew, hun, it's time to get up. It's almost 12:00 o'clock," she whispered.

He stirred just a hair and mumbled something inaudible.

"Drew! Wake up. You're wasting the day away." This time it was his dad, and Drew finally snapped up and out from under the covers.

"Alright, I'm up, I'm up," he grumbled with eyes still half asleep and hair in a tangle.

"Your brothers and sister are out swimming if you want to join them."

"Yeah, alright, I might do that." He yawned and laid his head back down on his paper-thin pillow.

"Or you can help me mow the lawn, it's up to you." His dad grinned.

At the sound of this, he sprung up and dashed for the clothesline where his swim trunks still hung from yesterday's swim. Mowing the lawn was the last thing he wanted to do in the tropical heat. Dario winked at Shelly, and she rolled her eyes with a smile.

Sody and Jamie each grabbed a tube and floated out to the middle of the small bay. Meanwhile, Keegan got too cold in the early June water and left to dry off. His brother and sister skirted past the lily pads and cabbage weeds to reach a spot where their feet didn't have to touch the slimy shoots which liked to tangle around ankles and toes. He glanced back at them and shivered his way back to the camper.

"Sody, you're going to get burnt," lectured Jamie. "Did you even put on any sunscreen?" She couldn't help but play mom. Jamie and Shelly were both worry warts.

"No, I tan easily. I'm not going to burn." He could feel his shoulders getting warm, but figured it was just from the heat of the day.

"If you say so."

"Hey Jamie . . ."

"Yeah?" She squinted over at Sody.

"If you had to pick your favorite part about summer, what would it be? And you can't say not being in school or that you get to relax. Everyone says that. If you really think about it, what's the best part?"

Jamie, just a year older than him, struggled with the question at first. She undoubtedly enjoyed not being in school and she certainly appreciated relaxing too.

After a moment of careful thought, she responded, "My favorite part of summer is magic."

"Magic. . . ? What magic? Like witch magic?"

"No. You know what I mean. Like fireworks, fireworks are magic. And sunsets too. The sky is always bursting with different colors each night and you never know how or why, it just is. I think campfires are magic too. Campfires always put people in a special mood and make them tell ghost stories and stuff."

Sody let all this soak in. He thought about all those things, and she was right, summer, without a doubt, seemed like magic to him too.

"Now it's my turn," huffed Jamie, startling Sody, who was lost deep in thought.

"Okay, shoot."

"What is your *least* favorite part about summer?"

Now that was a question he could answer. He had often pondered this question, starting at a young age. His least favorite part about anything was that it had to end. Sody thought about having to move away from his childhood home. He reflected upon all the summers previous which always ended too soon and about his favorite shoes that were never as good as the first week of wearing them.

"My least favorite part about summer is the thought that it might be the best summer I'll ever have and other ones in the future will never be as good as *this* one. Doesn't that scare you? That you might never have a better summer?"

"That is pretty scary," Jamie responded solemnly in almost a whisper as if to prevent the thought from becoming a possibility. She wondered if the magic of summer would always stay magic or if at some time that faded too, just like her memories of the old house would inevitably fade.

Their conversation was interrupted by their mom's voice calling to them from the shoreline.

"Kids! Come on in, there's watermelon." Her voice cut through the air, severing any further negative thoughts about summer.

The two raced back to shore on their tubes. They quickly passed some bulrushes and could see the sandy bottom below the water's surface. Sody knew the quickest way to swim with a tube was to point your back where you wanted to go and paddle with both arms in unison in big, drawn-out strokes like an eagle taking off from its perch.

Once at shore the tubes were tossed onto the grass, and they raced off for snacks and refreshments. Across the lake a tiny breeze picked up, just enough to ripple the stillness of the glass-like surface of the lake. The world once more began to stir. Dragonflies, acrobats of the sky, buzzed about in full force, hunting for an afternoon meal of mosquitoes and midges. Somewhere on the lake a lone loon sang a ghostly, wonderful song. Across the bay, smoke from the neighbor's campfire billowed up from behind the evergreens fencing the shoreline.

And just like that, the magic of summer was back.

CHAPTER 4

The Spirit of the North Wind

Sody's Grandma Joyce floated around the kitchen making lunch when the Fairbanks arrived. His grandparents lived on Lake Brushanti, in a quiet lake home tucked away neatly in the woods. Hot ham and cheese sandwiches and fresh watermelon were on the menu today. A simple lunch, but one of Sody's favorites. How did his grandma always pick the perfect melon? It must have been a trait all grandmothers were born with.

His grandma was petite and slightly plump. After all, you can't trust a skinny cook. A pair of reading glasses hung religiously from her neck on a gold-linked chain. She was eternally busy in the kitchen. Cooking, but not often cleaning. The house perpetually cluttered. Not dirty, but cluttered, and that was just fine. That is how it was and how it always had been and how it would always be.

After kicking his sandals off, Sody sprinted up the carpeted stairs to greet his grandma and grandpa. Before long, he and his siblings were stuffing themselves with endless hot ham and cheese sandwiches and the juiciest watermelon there ever was. The watermelon tasted like summer on the tongue, right down to the rind.

After they had all overfilled their stomachs, their grandma warned them about going swimming too soon after filling their bellies.

"You kids wait a little bit now before you go swimming. We don't need you getting cramped out in the lake."

"But grandma, it's so hot already. We'll just stay in the shallow water," replied Jamie.

"Fine, but only if your mom goes down to watch you all." she said, eyeing Shelly.

"I'll watch them, Joyce." their mom smiled. "Thank you so much for lunch. Kids, say thank you to your grandma."

She turned around to see the kids were already gone. Turning back to Grandma Joyce, she sighed, "Such great manners."

"They thanked me with their eyes and their smiles. I could tell. You have great kids, Shelly. And I have great grandkids. George and I always enjoy the company."

Outside not a cloud could be found in the baby blue sky. A southerly breeze whipped up short, choppy waves across the round lake and sent them crashing into the northern shoreline where grandma and grandpa's house sat perched on a small rise. Crab apple trees and birches dotted the meticulously trimmed yard. Sody's grandpa had retired three years ago and had since taken a particular interest in keeping his yard immaculate. The smell of fresh cut grass hovered thick in the stale summer air. A fragrance that never got old for the restless souls of summer.

"Drew!" yelled Sody.

The kids raced to the lake. It seems everything is a race when you are a kid. It was important to be the fastest, even if you had to give yourself a little head start. Drew had become an expert at this. He had somehow already snuck down to the lake and greased up the small aluminum water slide hanging off the end of the dock with water. *Come to think of it, Drew was never inside while they were eating lunch*, Sody thought to himself. His older brother could become invisible at will, a trait he desired to one day learn.

"What took ya so long?" Drew shouted as Sody careened out of the sauna that rested near the lake.

"I was hungry!"

"You're always hungry."

How completely true. Sody ate an abnormal amount of food, but one would never guess it. Drew and his friends had nicknamed him 'Bones' because he was as skinny as a skeleton.

Splash!

Sody 360'd off the end of the dock and let himself sink to the sandy bottom of Lake Brushanti. The cool water engulfed his body, lessening the heat of the fever hot sun. He opened his eyes underwater to see his younger brother, Keegan, launch towards him and do a jackknife.

Sploosh!

Keegan broke the surface of the choppy water and sank to the bottom, sending millions of tiny bubbles rising up around him, escaping to the top.

They swam, jumped off docks, floated on tubes in the hot sun, and played shark in the water until dinner called. This was a whole new world for Sody. Sure, he had been able to swim some when they would come out to visit his grandparents in the summers when they still lived in Togo, but now . . . now he could do this every day, all day if he really wanted to. On *two* different lakes! This was extraordinary. If he were back in Togo, he would be sweltering in the summer heat where his only escape involved running through the sprinkler in the backyard or getting an ice-cold popsicle from the freezer.

"Boys! No going out so far!" Came their grandma's voice from the second story deck. "You're not good enough swimmers for that."

She worried constantly about the safety of her grandkids and knew how to humble them as well. Sody, followed by Drew and Keegan, swam back closer to shore where Jamie stood making mini pots out of thick clay that she dug out of the lake. Sitting in the sun to dry, they looked like ancient artifacts, brittle and rugged and masterful.

"Hey, those look awesome Jamie. How do you make those?" Sody asked with honest curiosity.

"So, you have to start by grabbing a big handful of clay," she pointed at a spot in the lake where the shallow water had turned a muddy grey. "Then you just use your hands to form it like this."

Jamie displayed a clay bowl that looked like it had been spun on a potter's wheel. At that, Sody began working a ball of clay in a fevered attempt to create something as good as his sister's. He aimed to be the best at everything, but clearly pottery was not something he would excel at.

"Jamie, I'm awful at this, and you're really good. Here's what I made . . . er . . . tried to make." Sody brought his clay creation over to show his sister.

She let out a giggle at the sight of the clay bowl that looked like it had been stepped on and dropped, and then used as a football.

"Hey, at least you tried. That's all that really matters," she said seriously and set his pot next to the one's she already had drying.

A large cedar tree that loomed over the lake had a wooden swing their mother rocked back and forth on. It jutted out of the small hill that bordered the lake, leaning over the water and supplying anyone who swung a shelter from the sun. While watching Jamie and Sody make their pots, a giant ball of mud struck her.

"Bombs away!" Drew shouted from afar, and the softball sized mudball rocketed through the air.

Splat!

It smacked their mom right in the leg.

"Drew! Look what you did!" she shouted as she bolted up from the swing with mud splatter all over her shorts. "No more mudballs please." She marched up to the house after cleaning the muck off her thigh. No way she was going to stay down there in the middle of a mud fight.

"Sorry mom!"

Sploosh!

Another ball exploded just shy of where Sody and Jamie were standing in knee deep water, splashing them in the process. Drew didn't listen very well, and now that his mom left, he had free reign.

"Mud fiiight!" someone shouted, and then it was on.

It didn't take long before mud rained all over the shoreline. Drew slung a fastball towards Sody, who dove under the water just in time. Jamie knelt down behind him collecting mud when Drew's throw hit her square in the back.

"Sorry! That one was meant for Bones."

"Sure it was!" she exclaimed as she tossed one back at him.

Sody still had not surfaced and Drew started to worry. *Where is he? Is he okay?* Suddenly he got pulled underwater by his ankles and dragged to the sea floor, where Sody held him under as long as he could. But Drew was much stronger than Sody and soon escaped his brother's grasp. They both broke the surface at the same time, turning to each other and laughing for a second before grappling once more. In the meantime, Jamie and Keegan headed to shore to dry off. Shucking their towels in the wind, they shook off all the uninvited hitchhiker ants and sand.

Later that evening, Grandpa George drove down to the firepit on his patched up, rickety, green four-wheeler. He had gone up to the house to grab bug spray because the mosquitos, having sensed the setting of the sun, were already buzzing about in full force. The firepit sat near the edge of the lake on a small hill. The large rocks encircling it were charred-up on the inside, standing the tests of heat and time. An enormous, dead white pine loomed above the fire. It had lost its top half years prior to a lightning strike and now stood only a stark shard of the giant it once was.

The Fairbanks clan, one by one, settled into the seats surrounding the fire. The evening cooled as the sun slipped beneath the tips of the trees. Time for smores and fire roasted hot dogs and family. Time for magic.

Grandpa, after quieting the kids down, asked them if they wanted to hear a story.

Sody was the first to speak up, "Tell us about the Wiindigo, Grandpa."

Everyone turned to face Sody, appalled that he said the name out loud. The name of an ancient Ojibwe evil spirit. And to request a spirit story to be told out of season? It was unlike him, and unlike Ojibwe tradition.

His grandpa shifted uneasily in his chair while pondering Sody's request. "Now Sody, you know I'm not supposed to do that. I'm not supposed to tell spirit stories until wintertime. That is our way. To go against that would be to go against the Ojibwe spirits which we call the manidoog. And surely the manidoog would not take kindly."

"Come on Grandpa," coaxed Sody, "Just this one time. I'm sure the manidoog will be understanding."

If only they were.

There was a long pause before his grandpa finally answered.

"You know what, you are probably right." He stoked the fire with a long stick, sending plumes of sparks and smoke upward towards the stars. Grandpa George loved telling stories and was very good at it. He had a voice that hummed up and down like the ancient beat of a drum, the heartbeat of mother earth.

"When I was about your guys' age I walked down to this very spot. Except it was winter and back then this was all forest. I came searching for a man they called the Spirit Talker. It was believed he still lived in this area, but nobody had gone to see him in years. Those who saw him last said he had changed. Said the color in his eyes had left him. That he was sick, but not sick like the flu. Like he was possessed by a bad spirit."

Grandpa scanned his audience around the fire and cleared his throat.

"But I was desperate. I needed help to find my way in life. So, I went looking for the Spirit Talker, and after many hours searching I did find him . . . or rather, he found me. But he was no longer the Spirit Talker. The man I saw was no longer a man but a gaunt giant standing eight feet tall. His body was skeletal and ashy grey and smelled of decay and rot. His icy blue eyes were sunk into hollow sockets and the lips were no longer there so you could see his sharp teeth. The skin was taut against his bones and his face no longer looked human. At that moment I knew . . . the Spirit Talker had turned into a Wiindigo!"

At that very instant a log from the fire fell, sending hot sparks flying into the night air. Sody swore he saw a black shape trail the sparks but told himself it was only smoke. A loon cried out on the lake and the fine hair stood straight as nails on Sody's back. The loon too seemed to be listening, and perhaps it saw what Sody had seen.

His grandpa continued with the story. "I will only say the name once so as not to awaken it. From here on out, I will call it what many others have agreed to call it—the spirit of the north wind. It is said that spirits of the north wind will kill anybody who comes across their path, or worse, turn that person into one themselves. I was so scared I couldn't move. And it kept coming towards me. It breathed heavily like it had been running for days. Slowly it crept, because it knew I was too scared to run. Slowly, because it had no energy left to burn. See, we Ojibwe believe that spirits of the north wind feed on humans. But no matter how many they eat, they always crave more. They can never get enough to satisfy their extraordinary hunger. They are greed in the form of a monster."

"How did you survive?" interrupted Jamie with eyes as big as saucers.

"Please tell us," said Keegan, "Finish the storrry."

Sody sat back in the shadows, not sure if he wanted to hear more. Yet he stayed, frozen on the log that was his seat, listening intently to his grandpa. Waves from the lake whooshed into the shore and the sun set. Immediately a cold breeze whisked through the trees riddling Sody with goosebumps. It felt like winter, leaving a chill that shivered his bones. He let his imagination get away from him, sitting there, with trees all around, alone in the winter, with the spirit of the north wind looming over him.

"Okay, okay, but only 'cause you asked." Grandpa finally said. His voice carried them all away into the tale once more.

"As the evil spirit closed the distance, I finally got strength enough to run. I ran as fast as I could through knee deep snow, but no matter how fast I ran it kept gaining on me. It was so close to me I could almost taste its foul smell. Eventually, I came upon a clearing in the woods and made the mistake of looking back. My feet stumbled on a downed log, and I fell face first into the snow. I thought for sure I was a goner. That he was about to eat me or worse."

He paused for dramatic effect, the flames from the fire reflected eerily off his square spectacles.

"That he would turn *me* into one of his kind—a spirit of the north wind. But I was lucky that day. The good manidoog were on my side. My spirit bird, migizi, was there to help me. You all remember that migizi means eagle in Ojibwe, I hope. That migizi swooped down from the clouds and clawed at what was left of the spirit's eyes. I'll never forget the screams and yelps that followed. It gave me time to get away and that is how I survived to tell this tale. Never underestimate the power of the manidoog. The good ones or the bad ones."

The kids peered into the woods, hoping no spirit of the north wind would come on this night. They scooted closer to the fire for protection.

"Did you ever see it again?" Sody finally spoke. He started to shake. From the cold or from fear he was not sure. *Why was it so cold all of a sudden?*

"Oh yes. I did see another one, years later. Its icy blue eyes burned a hole in my soul. Something I cannot unsee," finished Grandpa George solemnly.

"G-grandpa. . ." Sody stammered, "Do you think that they are still around?"

He peered into his grandfather's eyes, needing closure.

"I don't think so, Sody. Well at least I don't believe they are. They seem to have disappeared and no one has reported seeing one for a long time. Although it is said they still sometimes come around at night when there is a blue moon," he fibbed seriously.

"When is the next blue moon?"

"TONIGHT!" yelled Grandpa.

Everyone screamed, including the kids' parents and grandma. Sody and Jamie fell backwards off their seats. Jamie got up and nuzzled next to her mom.

"It's okay hun, it's just a story," her mom cooed while rubbing Jamie's back. "No it's not, it's reeeal," wailed Jamie.

"Jamie, dear. I'm sorry. It is indeed just a story. I didn't mean to frighten you . . . at least not quite so much," her grandpa said with a mischievous grin hidden behind a shadow.

The whole way home Sody thought about the spirit's icy blue eyes and he wondered if the customer he saw at the cafe had blue eyes underneath that hood. He could feel eyes looking at him, piercing him. *From where?* Sody looked around frantically. He could not shake the feeling. The spirit of the northwind had

Sody in its grasp. One had come out on this blue moon, just like his grandpa said it would and now it was out for blood. Of this, Sody was sure, and the spirit had chosen him.

As the Suburban lumbered down the dirt road back to the camper, the road became narrower, and the trees grew in close. A full moon floated like a ghost atop the pines ahead. Sody couldn't tell if it was actually a blue moon or not, but he convinced himself it must be. They drove right towards the imposing ghost-white orb when something slunk out of the ditch in front of the Suburban and trundled across the road. As swift as it appeared, it disappeared. For just a split second the beam of the headlights silhouetted it against the road. *Was it a wolf? A bear? Could it have been a spirit of the north wind? Who could know?* As for Sody, he was certain what he saw had not been a natural being. He looked around at his parents and siblings and nobody appeared to have seen what he saw crossing the road, so he didn't bother to ask them. He shivered uncontrollably, eyes opening wider as the road got narrower.

CHAPTER 5

Blueberry Picking

A little more than a week after his grandpa's spirit story, Sody could finally sleep through the night again. The first few nights he did not rest a wink. A gripping fear held him tightly and prevented any rest because of nightmares so scary he didn't even *want* to sleep. He dared not tell his parents for fear of getting his grandpa in trouble. After all, he had only been telling a story, right? And the new feeling that haunted him, the overwhelming anxiousness, that was normal too, right? Drew seemed to sleep just fine. So did Jamie. And Keegan never acted as if the spirit bothered him. Maybe he wasn't normal. Maybe he was different.

Sody *felt* different. He had always been full of confidence and joy. But lately he felt strange, like his impenetrable armor had been chinked. Would he ever be the same?

"Sody, get up," whispered his mom, gently shaking him, "I'm going to make breakfast."

The bed Sody slept on in the camper doubled as the dining room table. The pink cushions folded up and turned into benches and the middle of the "bed" stood up to form the table.

He was just short enough for this makeshift bed that he didn't have to bend his legs at all to fit. The perfect size for him and his flannel sleeping bag and pillow.

"What are you making?" Sody grumbled, wiping the sleep from his eyes. A sleep long overdue.

"Pancakes."

"With blueberries?"

"Of course. Speaking of blueberries, we are going to need to do some picking today to get some more. We are just about out. Would you like to come with me and your sister today? Your grandma showed me a secret spot not too far from here a long time ago. We could go check it out."

"I guess so." Sody shrugged his shoulders as if to say, 'What choice do I have?'

His dad planned on taking Drew and Keegan over to see their new house being built and figured to be gone most of the day. Sody refused to go with them because he wanted the new house to be a surprise when it was complete. So, he could either go blueberry picking with his mom and sister or sit at the camper all by himself, and the latter did not sound very appealing. Especially since the spirit of the northwind could still be out there lurking in the woods. He shuddered at the thought.

Even after being crammed in the old camper for three weeks, none of the kids had any major quarrels with each other yet. In fact, their mom thought to herself, it seemed that they were bickering even less than usual. Maybe the fresh air helped, or maybe the freedom the kids had in the woods, but they all seemed to be getting along quite well, much to her delight.

"After picking, maybe I'll take you both to the spring." Shelly said to Jamie and Sody, who were cutting into their fresh blueberry pancakes.

Sody looked up from his plate with a mouthful of pancake. "The spring? What's that?"

"Oh . . . you two have never been there, have you? Well, a spring is a spot in the ground where water flows to the surface. And there is one just down the road from the berry patch. Since it's going to be so hot today it will be a nice break after we are done picking."

Jaime set her cup of orange juice down. "That sounds cool."

"Can we go after breakfast? I want to go before it gets too hot, mom. And can I have another pancake, please?" Sody asked enthusiastically.

"Of course you can." His mom flopped another hot cake onto Sody's plate, thankful her son finally appeared to be in a good mood again.

"Don't bears eat blueberries?" inquired Sody.

His dad spoke up from his perch on the couch. He was certainly enjoying his two-week vacation from work. "Oh yes, they *love* blueberries! You will probably see one today so make sure you can run fast . . . or at least faster than your mom or sister."

Sody turned in his seat at the table to face his dad and rolled his eyes.

"Daaad! That's not funny. I'm being serious. Can't they run super-fast?"

"Yes, they can, but don't worry, you probably won't actually see one. They are more scared of you than you are of them," he said casually. "Unless they have cubs around. In that case you better start praying."

His dad was reading the newspaper. His only way of keeping up with what was going on out in the *real* world since they no longer had TV or internet. Grandpa was generous enough to bring the paper over from his house after he finished with them. Although the newspapers were always a week old or better, his dad did not complain.

"Alright, Dario, that's enough." Shelly interjected, hands on her hips. "Quit trying to scare the kids. Shouldn't you be leaving now anyways?"

She rolled her eyes just like Sody had and set her pancake spatula on the counter. The family rolled their eyes at Dario an awful lot. He liked being the trickster.

He finally set the newspaper down. "Just trying to teach them a thing or two about bears is all." He heaved himself up from the couch and walked out of the camper into the mugginess of another midsummer morning.

A smell lingered in the stale air outside the camper. A fragrance of dried grass and dead pine needles and the leftovers of last night's campfire. Sody hopped outside into the gravel lot and inhaled a deep breath of the spice of summer. The camper sat surrounded by trees on all sides except for the front which had the grandest view of the lake just one hundred feet from the camper's steps. A grove of enormous white pines lined the shoreline like skyscrapers. And there, in the middle, sat the Fairbanks' firepit which was an abandoned rim of an old dump truck, long retired from the ore mines of Minnesota's Iron Range.

Sody watched Keegan cast a fishing line off the dock. The line glistened in the sun for a moment before resting on the still surface of the lake. He loved to fish just as much as Sody. It was a hobby they both enjoyed doing together, even if it often turned into a competition of who could catch the biggest fish. He pondered the craft of his cast. Keegan, only eight-years-old, could handle a fishing rod as well as he could, maybe better, he admitted to himself. It was truly an artform too often under-appreciated—the dexterity of casting. A sculptor can create a statue out of marble; a fisherman can make a lure dance in the air, skip across the water and land right under an overhanging log where a hungry fish lay in wait.

Sody smiled at witnessing his younger brother becoming a master. He looked on for a few more minutes and watched Keegan pull up a half dozen small sunfish, each one lifted out of the water and dangled on the end of the fishing pole, spinning slowly like a floating dreidel before being plucked off the hook and tossed back into the blue-green water. Keegan looked back and noticed Sody watching him. A grin spread across his face, then he turned slowly back to the lake, brought his pole back, and swept another elegant cast.

Later that day, with the sun hanging high, Jamie and his mom were crouched over the bountiful blueberry patch. The patch edged the side of a dirt road and extended to the tree line at the heart of the Chippewa State Forest. They picked handfuls of enormous berries and set them in their ice cream pails that were filling quickly. Their mom swatted a deer fly off her forearm.

"Jamie, where's your brother?" she asked. "I'm about ready to go. Still wanna go to the spring?"

"I haven't seen him in a while. Thought he was by you. And yes, I still wanna go! I'm melting over here," Jamie replied, wiping her forehead where her curly brunette hair clung like glue to her face.

"Sody! We're ready to go!" yelled his mom. It seemed to her she was always yelling for him. Sody loved to go on little adventures, especially in uncharted territory.

"Almost ready!" came a voice from somewhere in the forest on the other side of the dirt road.

Sody was knelt down under a grove of mature spruce trees, his ice cream pail nearly empty. He poked at an enormous ant hill and watched as thousands of the tiny insects scrambled to repair the spots he poked. They were fascinating. Fast and strong and organized. They had created a three-foot-high ant-hill in the middle of nowhere. *How many ants are in this colony? It must be over a million,* Sody pondered when he heard the jerky rumble of the car engine start up. He grabbed his pail and hopped out to the road where his mom and sister waited impatiently.

His mom couldn't be mad though. Not after seeing the sparkling curiosity in her son's eyes.

"Ready to go to the spring?"

"Let's do it!" yipped Sody, crawling into the back seat of the blood red, rusty Dodge Stratus.

They headed down a winding path bordered closely on both sides by spruce plantations. They rolled their windows down and turned the music up. *Highway Man* played over the speakers thanks to the burned CD from Grandpa George. Earlier that summer the air conditioning unit on the car had quit working. Having the windows down created just enough air flow to suppress the hot and humid summer air.

His mom slowly pulled to the edge of the road and parked the car. "Alright, here we are."

Jamie looked around questioningly. "We are? But I don't see anything?" She looked out in front of the car. On either side stood nothing but trees lining the sides of the road. She was skeptical.

"Just get out and follow me," said their mom.

They left the windows down on the car and stepped off the road, walking through a ditch towards the woods. Just short of the tree line, hidden beneath long grass and dead leaves, was an old sheet of metal laid across the ground. Their mom grabbed at a corner and lifted the metal up and set it aside. Sody and Jamie peeked down to see crystal clear water in a little pool below the ground. A small hole in the earth is all there was. They expected something much bigger, yet the spring still left them staring in awe.

"Try some," encouraged their mom.

Grabbing the plastic water bottles they carried with, they dunked them in the water, filled each to the top and drank deeply from the spring. Sody took a sip at first. So fresh and so cold, like ice on a fresh burn. January-midnight cold. He tipped the bottle back a tad more and inhaled a giant gulp. A potion, a blend of northern Minnesota snow and glacier ice melted to just above freezing. It was *magic*.

Sody finally quit drinking long enough to talk, "Mom . . . this is amazing. How did you find out about this?"

"Your grandma showed me this spot years ago," she reminisced. "Your grandparents used to have a cabin on this lake too and your dad came to this very spot when he was your age. This spring has been here for ages, for hundreds of years. Maybe more."

"That's so cool! I want to come here more often," said Sody in between gulps. "It's like a wishing well for the parched. And boy was I parched."

"We sure can, hun. Next time we will bring your brothers too. They haven't seen this spot either. Don't tell anybody about this though. It can be our little secret. Our own little wishing well."

Sody and Jamie's eyes twinkled—a secret. They loved secrets. Secrets are arcane promises, mysterious under-the-table knowledge that no one else knows about. That is the magic of secrets. You know something others don't. And that is why, for kids, some secrets are so easy to keep.

On the way back to the camper, with bellies full of glacial cold water, their mom asked, "How many berries did you end up with, Sody?"

"I nearly filled my pail!" Jamie boasted from her seat in the front of the car before Sody could respond.

"I . . . uh . . . I got a decent amount." Sody replied with cheeks flushing red.

His mom peeked over her shoulder and saw Sody's nearly empty bucket and shook her head smiling.

"You little brat. I'm not going to take you picking anymore if you're going to eat all the ones you pick."

This was just fine for Sody, who that day discovered he didn't care a thing about picking blueberries. It was grueling work sitting under a hot sun all the while getting bitten by bugs and flies and spiders, and that just didn't seem worth it to him.

"Okay," he muttered, "sorry, Mom."

In a high branch of a basswood tree on the lot where the Fairbanks family's new house was being erected sat a bald eagle, perched at the apex near the shoreline of Lake Makwa. She seemed to be overseeing the construction, but more realistically was probably waiting for her chance to swoop down and grab an all too careless fish from the lake. Her presence was enough to quiet the workers, however, while they gazed up at her grace—a image of wonder. A primal species at the top of the food chain. A symbol of freedom to many, and much, much more than just a symbol to some.

"Migizi," their dad whispered to Drew and Keegan while looking up at the majestic bird. "Remember, that is the Ojibwe word for bald eagle."

"Migizi," repeated Keegan.

"Oh yeah." Drew gazed up in absolute admiration. "I remember grandpa teaching us that."

"It's a good sign it is here. It has come to bring good fortune," added the boys' dad. He shielded his eyes from the sun's glare. "Eagles are the messengers of the Ojibwe people."

The sound of a nail gun disrupted the silence and the eagle finally leapt from its throne, soaring low above the surface of the lake, racing its reflection on the water before disappearing behind a point that jutted out into the lake. The workers were back at it, busy finishing up the frame for the house. To Keegan and Drew, it looked like a skeleton. The bare bones of their new home. A concrete slab had been poured a few weeks earlier and now the house looked to be really coming along. It was a process, Dario knew, but he was ready for it to be finished and to move out of the camper. He enjoyed living in the camper because of the close proximity it had with nature, but he would have that same closeness in their new home without being crammed into a thirty-foot tin can.

He made his way over to the house to talk with the carpenters while the two boys ran down to the lake playing fetch with their dog Mocha.

"How goes the battle, Scott?" shouted Dario over the sound of the air compressor that powered the nail gun.

"She's goin'!" Scott yelled back and shut the compressor down, shaking Dario's hand.

"It's looking good. Nice to see it start to take shape."

"Agreed, she's gonna be a looker when we finish up with her," he replied, referring to the house.

Dario rapped his knuckles on a 2x4 and peered around at his dream home coming to fruition. "Any estimate on when it'll be done?" He smiled proudly. "I know it's early and all, but I can't help but ask."

"Most likely the end of August. At least that is the plan, barring any major setbacks or bad weather."

"Perfect. Just in time before school starts for the young ones."

"Exactly," replied Scott, driving a nail into another 2x4.

"Well, I'll let you guys be. The wife made you some beverages." Dario set down a large pitcher of lemonade and plastic cups on the makeshift sawhorse table, then walked down to the shoreline where Drew was now teaching Keegan how to properly skip rocks.

"You want to find the flattest ones," explained Drew. "The flatter they are, the better they will glide on top of the water."

After they each gathered a handful of skippers, Drew continued with his coaching, "Now you want to bend sort of low, so you are closer to the water. Then you wind up and throw it side arm. It's a lot different than you would throw a baseball. Here, watch this."

Drew wound up and slung a rock that skipped once, twice, three times and finally sank after the fourth skip.

"That was pretty sweet!" exclaimed Keegan.

"Now it's your turn."

Keegan mimicked his brother's motions and flung an expert toss. His rock skipped six times before losing momentum and sinking.

Drew gazed on in awe, a little jealous of his brother's natural knack for skipping.

"Beginner's luck," said Drew with arms crossed, "bet you can't do that again."

Keegan wound up once more and let fly another rock. This time it skipped not six but seven times. Drew was dumbfounded. It quickly became a competition of who could get the most skips.

In the meantime, their dad strolled around the yard, hands in pockets, inspecting the land. Just a few months ago the entire lot had been covered with trees. You couldn't even see the lake from the road. Now it was cleared with grass growing and a few beautiful basswoods and maples left sprinkled about the yard. He smiled at the sight of it all. He envisioned where the dock would go and the swimming raft that he planned to build for the kids. Perhaps he would construct a fish cleaning house near the shore, or a sauna . . . or both! The possibilities were nearly endless.

A sauna, Dario contemplated, yes, a sauna is a must. He and the kids loved taking saunas. At their home in Togo they had had one in the basement. The walls were sided with rough cut cedar that emitted a wonderful, earthy fragrance when heated up. There was a large, rectangular stove in the corner and on it were grapefruit-sized rocks stacked high to hold heat.

In the winter, Dario and all the kids would cram into the sauna. He would tell them stories of how he grew up in the tall, yellow house next door and about the adventures he had as a kid with his dog, Blanca. After the stories ended, they would all run upstairs and out onto the deck into the deep cold of the winter nights. Steam would rise off them like boiling pots, up into the air, disappearing somewhere among the starry sky. Dario told them it was impurities leaving their bodies which his children believed because after they always felt relaxed and fresh and renewed afterwards.

He, of course, missed the old home in Togo. They all did in fact. A lot of memories were made there in the ten years they owned it. It was where Dario watched his kids grow up. Where he taught them how to ride a bike and throw a football. However, there were still many things left to teach his kids at the new home. How to drive a boat. How to build a proper campfire. How to do a melon off the raft. A melon was an upside-down cannonball, his favorite move.

"What do you think, boys?" said Dario as he walked up to where Keegan and Drew were still skipping rocks.

"This is awesome!" cried Keegan.

"It's a pretty cool spot. Nowhere to skate though," said Drew somewhat unimpressed, thinking about the park he used to ride his skateboard in with his friends. "How much longer till we can move in? The camper is starting to get a little old. No offense."

"I just talked to Scott, one of the carpenters, and he said they should be done by the end of July."

"Soo . . . basically another month then? Dad, I'm gonna go crazy out there. We're all so crammed in that tin can and I don't get any privacy."

Dario sensed his son's disappointment. "I know, I know. But it's only a month. It will go by quick kid, trust me," he pleaded. He knew exactly where Drew was coming from. After all, he was sixteen once, even if Drew didn't realize it.

"You should take the car and go see your friends back in Togo one of these days. Get away for a little while, it might do ya some good."

"You'd let me do that?" Drew couldn't believe it.

"Absolutely, just let me know when you want to go. You could give them a call on grandpa and grandma's phone if you'd like since we don't have a phone out there."

"Thanks dad!" Upon hearing this news, Drew gave his dad a hug, something he rarely did. He wasn't much for showing affection, but at this instant he couldn't help it.

There had been no contact between him and his friends all summer. The Fairbanks were officially off the grid and had been for a month. Their mother did have an ancient Nokia phone probably made in the early Cretaceous period, but there was no reception within twenty miles of the camper anyway. They could still play snake on it though! When they needed to call somebody, they had to drive ten miles to the grandparent's house to use their landline. Their dad loved the fact they didn't have regular phone service. He enjoyed not having to take calls from work every day. It was more peaceful this way.

It was how summer should be.

CHAPTER 6
The Fort

Sody peered up at the relentless sun. It wasn't even noon and the thermometer already read eighty-five degrees. He took a sip of water from his canteen and continued hacking away at a balsam tree with his hatchet. Keegan stood nearby with an old machete his grandpa had given him, hacking off the branches of the trees Sody chopped down. They were both shirtless, wearing basketball shorts and open toed sandals. If their parents caught them dressed like this, they would be dead meat. *You could chop a toe off*, his mom would scream in a hysteria if she saw them, and then they would be grounded forever.

"Hey Keegs, watch out. This one is about to go," said Sody, while pushing on the tree he notched with his hatchet.

Creeeeeak!

The tree groaned before breaking at the notch. They watched it fall silently before crashing into the forest floor.

"TIMBERRRR!" they both yelled in unison.

They felt like loggers of the north country. There were trees and limbs and wood chips littering the ground all around them. Balsams and aspens and spruces scattered every which way.

"Do you think this is enough yet?" panted Keegan.

"Yeah, I think so." Sody scanned the area with hands on his hips. "At least for now. We may need to chop some more down later."

The two boys each grabbed a tree and drug it over to the spot where they had started building a fort. Their cousin, Jackson Dougherty, stood up on the small platform they'd erected in between three large balsam trees, nailing in a final crooked floorboard. The floor of the fort consisted of a patchwork of 2x4's, tongue and groove and even small chunks of plywood, any leftover lumber they could steal from Jackson's dad. It sat five feet off the forest floor, held together with nails and hope, with a small makeshift ladder tacked into one of the trees to get up.

"Well guys, it's a start!" Jackson exclaimed with a smile stretching from ear to ear.

Jackson was Jamie's age and loved building forts as much as Sody and Keegan. He, like Sody, wore glasses, and it was a good thing they did since wood chips and nails flew through the air like shrapnel while they worked.

"It's taking shape, that's for sure," replied Sody, wiping the sweat from his forehead. "Hey Jackson, what do you think about making another level on the fort? Like up above the one you're standing on."

"That would be awesome! Let's try it."

The boys set to work, hacking up the logs they gathered into pieces that would reach from one tree to the next. Their fort was built into three trees that stood apart from each other in the shape of a scalene triangle. This meant all their wood had to be cut into odd lengths and sizes. They didn't use a measuring tape, so two of them held the logs up between two trees while the other hacked off the end with a bow saw. This seemed to work just fine, and why would they need a tape measure when they could just do it their way?

A light bulb went off in Keegan's head. "You know what else we should do?"

"What's that?" asked Jackson.

"We should build a fire pit. And get rocks from the gravel pit and use them to make a ring."

"Heck ya! That's a great idea, Keegs." Sody hee-hawed.

They imagined they were architects and carpenters and loggers. And in a way they were. Surely you don't need a tape measure to be a carpenter or a chainsaw to be a logger or a computer design to be an architect. They were kids, they could be anything. They were endless possibilities waiting to become.

Keegan moseyed off down the trail they had made through the woods to grab a spade shovel for digging out the fire pit. They weren't more than fifty yards from the camper, yet the forest stood so thick you couldn't see it, not even from atop the fort platform.

"This is perfect, my mom and dad probably don't even know we are back here." Sody boasted to Jackson.

"Doubtful. Let's keep it that way. I don't think your parents would be too happy if they knew we were chopping down all these trees."

The two boys sat on the platform of their fort, looking out at the sparkling lake. Sweat poured off of them and dirt, pine needles and leaves clung to their damp skin. Their arms and legs were full of scrapes from tree branches and nails, but they smiled. All was well at the lake. That was until Keegan came back with more than just a shovel.

He wore a big, proud grin on his face followed in close pursuit by his dad. Sody and Jackson shot him a dirty look as if to say, "Are you crazy?" but it was too late. Keegan ignored them. He wasn't aware that what they were doing might not be received well by their parents.

"What do you think, Dad?" Keegan exclaimed with arms outstretched towards the fort. Dario scanned around for a while showing no expressed emotion. Yet. He wore his orange Hawaiian shirt unbuttoned paired with blue swim shorts. Sody thought he looked almost relaxed.

"Sweet, guys!" said their dad enthusiastically after a painful silence. "Nice job on the fort. And I see you're cutting down some trees. That's okay, but just be careful and make sure not to go past this blue tape."

He pointed at a tree with a blue ribbon hanging from it. "This is the edge of our property so don't cut trees on the other side of it. Cool fort though. I remember when I was your guys' age and my friends and I would build forts all the time too. It's a lot of fun."

Jackson and Sody stared blankly. *What? We aren't in trouble?*

"Er . . . thanks Dario, we . . . we were hoping you would like it." stammered Jackson.

"Well I'm gonna go swimming. Do you guys want to join me?" said Dario, pointing over his shoulder through the woods to the beach. "It's getting pretty hot out here. Jamie is going to come too."

"Yeah . . . sure thing!" replied Sody, still slightly in shock.

Dario headed back down the path towards the camper, whistling on his way. Sody and Jackson gazed at each other with bulging eyes.

"Phew . . . talk about a close call. I thought he was going to be *livid*," murmured Sody.

"You're telling me," said Jackson.

"I knew he would think it was *cool*," finished Keegan before chasing after his dad.

The following day the three boys found their way back to their fort once more. Jackson and Keegan were busy digging out the fire pit when they noticed Sody trundling awkwardly through the woods with a wheelbarrow heaped with scrap wood.

"Holy man! Where did you get all that?" Jackson yipped with eyes as big as dinner plates.

"Grandpa is at the camper. He brought a bunch of wood for us. Said there was even more where this came from!" answered Sody.

"What's the catch?" Keegan asked, eyebrows raised to his hairline.

"There is no catch. Although dad said he wanted to use some of the better stuff to build a doghouse for Mocha, that still leaves us with plenty of wood to build our second story!"

"Well, let's get to it. Keegan, you keep doing the pit. We'll keep working on the base for the second story," said Jackson, one hand on a shovel and the other on his hip. A city worker in the making.

Jackson climbed up onto the first platform while Sody handed him balsam poles to use as the frame.

"Alright, now come up here and help me tack these babies in, Sody," Jackson grunted, "I'm not sure if we are going to be able to do this with just us two though . . . and Keegan is probably too short. Any chance Drew would want to help?"

"Maybe . . . put that log down for now," Sody replied, setting the wheelbarrow down. "I'll go ask him quick. Hopefully he's up. He usually sleeps until noon." He rolled his eyes, walking back to the camper.

It was nearing noon and the first overcast day in weeks. Finally, a break from the sweltering July heat. A blessing of clouds and cooler weather. But this would prove to only be a front of the weather yet to come.

Drew sat on the pink couch eating corn pops out of a Styrofoam bowl. He was the only one inside the camper. He had the A/C cranked on high while everybody else was outside.

The camper door flew open. "Drew. . ." panted Sody, "Can you help us with something on our fort?"

"Your fort?" Drew answered after choking down a spoonful of cereal. "Sure thing. What do you need help with?"

"Wellll, we're trying to build another story onto it. But Jackson and I can't do it ourselves, and Keegs is too short. It won't take long, I swear."

"No problem. I'll be right over after I finish this cereal."

"Thanks Drew!" Sody slammed the camper door shut before he could answer and shot off like a rocket back to the fort. It was a miracle the camper door was still on its hinges after all the abuse it took from the Fairbanks family.

Soon enough, Drew made his way down the narrow trail that wound through the woods to the fort. He noticed the area was full of poison ivy and wiped his brow with relief that he wore jeans. His brothers and Jackson on the other hand, were not.

"Holy smokes! This is pretty cool guys," said Drew as he entered the clearing.

"Come on up here," Jackson gestured to the platform. "We'll hold the logs while you pound them into the trees."

Drew shimmied up the ladder and onto the platform. Jackson and Sody hoisted up the balsam poles and Drew set to work with the hammer. It didn't take long before the three poles were up. Drew could pound nails better than most carpenters.

"Thanks, Drew," muttered Sody.

"No problem, this is going to look sweet when it's all done. Mind if I stick around and help you guys out?"

"Not at all, that would be great," chirped Jackson.

Drew got to work building the ladder higher so it could reach the next level. He quickly tacked in five more steps to the side of the tree. It was a thing of rugged beauty. A portal to the skies. A stairway to heaven.

Sody grabbed a crooked board from the pile of scrap wood heaped next to the fort and handed it up to Jackson standing on the first level. Jackson then passed it off to Drew who teetered at the top of the ladder with one arm wrapped around the tree. The first board of the floor was the hardest since he had to hammer it in while standing on the ladder. Drew leaned against the balsam tree for support and pounded the board into the smaller balsam poles that stretched across to the other two trees.

Meanwhile, Keegan huffed and puffed near his freshly dug fire pit. It took him the better part of an hour to shovel the small pit out. The endless trees surrounding them had long roots that crisscrossed the ground beneath and he had to chop each root out with the edge of his shovel. Now just a few large rocks to make up the ring around the pit and it would finally be complete. He wiped the sweat from his forehead and leaned on his shovel to gaze up at his older brother, Drew. He must have been fifteen feet up in the air, standing on a skinny "step" that was attached to the tree with a few measly nails. Keegan smiled. *There is no fear when you are young. Drew must still be a kid,* he thought, *or maybe he is just a little crazy.* Either way, he admired his brother's reckless bravery.

"Toss me up another one, boys," Drew shouted down from his perch. He was very technical and precise, or as precise as you can be without a tape measure or level. He made sure each board fit properly and when he finished with the second story platform it looked a sight better than the first. He even put in the trapdoor that Jackson and Sody had requested after borrowing a couple hinges from his dad's shed.

"I think it's done. Wanna come up and check it out?"

All three boys raced up to the second story. Jackson hoisted himself up through the trapdoor while Keegan chased Sody up the ladder. The view at the top was far more spectacular than anything they could have imagined. They were up in the clouds. On top of the world. Kings of the forest. If anyone came through the woods they would look like tiny ants from this height, so far below, so little, so insignificant.

"Hey Drew," Sody spoke up with a small crack in his voice. "Thanks for helping us. It looks really great."

"Yeah, thanks Drew!" added Jackson.

"No problem, guys. Glad I could help. Pretty cool view I'd say."

"Yeah, it is," finished Keegan, wiping his brow. "I don't think I've ever been up this high. It's kind of scary, but really cool. No one can touch us up here. We must be a hundred feet up."

"Hundred feet you think?" Drew chuckled a little, "Something like that Keegs . . . something like that. Hey, anyone have any water?"

Sody shook his canteen before opening the lid and tipped it upside down. Not a drop. Bone dry.

Drew eyed the canteen, his lips dry as the Mojave. "In that case, I'm gonna head back to the camper and grab a drink."

One by one they clambered down the ladder back to reality. Up top they were immortal, but down on the forest floor it was another story. The heat seemed magnified among the thick forest air. Horse flies and deer flies gravitated to the sweat perspiring from their bodies. Arms were flailing, swatting the winged pests off each other's backs. Sody scratched at his leg. It was unbearably itchy for some reason.

It had been four days since building the second story of the fort, but none of the boys had gone back. Nor would they for quite some time. Their mom sat at the table playing rummy with Jamie.

"Sody, you have to quit itching or it's going to get even worse," his mom said as she laid down four kings.

"Easy for you to say, *mom*. You don't have poison ivy. And plus, it feels *so* good to scratch it."

"You know," she replied nonchalantly, looking at her cards. "That poison ivy can spread to more places than just your legs." Sody's eyes doubled in size. He quit scratching immediately. She continued, "That's what I thought. I'll run to the hospital today and get you some steroid cream. Looks to me like that stuff isn't going away anytime soon."

"Thanks, mom. You're the best," grunted Sody, fighting the urge to scratch at the poison ivy that had spread up his calves and all the way to his knees.

"You're welcome, but no going back to the fort until your dad gets rid of the rest of that poison ivy. Can't believe you kids didn't notice it in those woods. It was everywhere."

"Guess we found out the hard way."

"Hey, Sody," said Jamie from behind the bench seat.

"Yeah?"

"*I* didn't get poison ivy." She stretched out the 'I' for a full second before turning around in her seat and sticking her tongue out at Sody.

Instead of fighting a battle he knew he wouldn't win, Sody curled up on the remarkably stiff couch and dozed off.

And then he dreamt of it again. The spirit of the north wind. From his grandfather's story. Its presence chilled his entire body. Gripping. Suffocating. The spirit was powerful beyond belief, but only when the power was given to it. They came about when humans were living in excess. When someone had much but still wanted more. Spirits of the north wind fed on sadness, fear, and most of all, on doubt. Sody never physically saw it in the dreams, but he could feel it . . . lurking in the shadows, radiating with a twisted aura, waiting for its next move. It was crafty, and cunning, and dangerous. Bright storm clouds always raged in these dreams. Each time it appeared to be closer. And Sody knew the spirit was in the storm. Waiting for him. Hungry.

A voice whispered to him, *don't let it in.* And then another voice, *Shhhh, you have nothing to fear. Listen to me and I will make your life easier.*

The second voice sounded more like a hoarse hiss. But it appeared friendly, at least it seemed that way. Sody moved closer to the second voice. It felt like he was being pulled that way. He got very close.

Yes, you're almost here . . . Come on now, yes. You're right where I WANT YO. . .

Sody snapped awake. He was freezing. Shivering. Nearly hypothermic.

"Hun . . . are you okay?" His mom stood over him.

"Fine. J . . . ju . . . just fine. Can you grab me a blanket?"

"Sody, it's a sauna in here. We don't even have the A/C on."

"Right," answered Sody, still shivering, "I'm fine. Just a bad dream I guess."

She eyed him suspiciously. "If you say so. We're going outside if you care to join."

"Yeah, okay. I'll be out later."

His mom and Jamie popped open the screen door of the camper and made their way down to the lake. Sody stayed in bed, laying on his back and looking up at the empty ceiling. *It was only a dream,* he kept telling himself. *It was only a dream.*

CHAPTER 7

Ringleader Road

"Sody, you can't always get what you want. Sometimes you have to settle for something else." His dad lectured his thirteen-year-old who vehemently disagreed with him.

The two sat at the small dining room table in the camper eating cereal, and Sody just finished *telling* his dad he was going exploring by himself to go on his vision quest. His mom and dad were getting ready to run into town to pick-up groceries and denied Sody's request because their son was not ready for his vision quest, or so they thought.

Why can't you always get what you want? If you want something bad enough, Sody thought, *then surely it is okay to not follow other people's advice all the time.* He agreed with most of his dad's judgment, but on this topic he certainly did not.

"I still think you're wrong," said Sody, crossing his arms. "I'm old enough to go on my vision quest. I have a compass and everything. I'm not going to get lost."

His dad listened patiently and decided his son made a good point. "Perhaps you are right. But you are forgetting that the world isn't perfect. The world doesn't always revolve around what you want. Sometimes you just have to trust us and listen to us. No going out in the woods alone, it's too dangerous. What if you come across a bear? Or you get turned around in the woods?"

"I wouldn't get turned around. I would keep the lake in view the whole time. I'm not a little kid anymore!" Sody fired back a bit more hotly than he intended, before opening the door and walking outside. He learned a lot from his dad, but he wanted to have more freedom and to find his purpose. His dad rushed out of the camper in hot pursuit.

"Don't walk away from me when I'm talking to you. You're getting a little too big for your britches. No means no, and that's final."

Sody felt his temper flaring up and found no way to control it. "I wish I had a different dad! You don't let me do anything."

He knew this wasn't true. His parents actually gave him quite a lot of freedom.

Dario's stomach dropped. That one hurt. He looked down at the ground and walked back into the camper, not knowing how to reply.

Sody was sick and tired of hearing what he could and could not do. It was like the saying "You can't have your cake and eat it too." He heard it a few times growing up and loathed it. Whoever came up with that was a sore loser. One most certainly could have their cake and eat it too, and he intended to. He felt bad about what he said to his dad. It wasn't true, but he was too stubborn to apologize. He would do it later. When he got back. Yes, he would apologize then. What he didn't know was that he might never get that chance.

In a world where ninety-nine percent of people are taught at a young age that in fact, some things *are* impossible, he wanted to be the one percent. The one percent who disagreed that you had to settle for anything less than what you dreamed of as a kid. And so, at age thirteen, Sody Fairbanks set his sails for greatness. He would go on his vision quest, even if he wasn't ready. Like a bird unfledged, he knew his inaugural journey would be met with obstacles, but no obstacle was too great to hinder his promise to himself: to pursue his dreams and hopefully, with a bit of luck, inspire others to follow theirs. What he didn't know, what no young person is aware of, is that the mightiest obstacle is in your own head.

His parents headed out to the silver Suburban and fired up the engine. They didn't notice any sign of Sody. Dario looked around for a while, checking the dock and new fort, trying to find him and say he was sorry and that he would help him with his vision quest someday soon, when he was ready. But he was nowhere to be found. He admitted to himself that maybe *he* wasn't the one who was ready for his son to become a man. For in Ojibwe culture, the vision quest was a time where boys became men by embarking on a solitary journey into the wilderness in search of a spiritual awakening. A place to leave behind distractions and focus on what their purpose in life was to be. He quarreled with the idea, knowing he had gone on his vision quest around the same age. *I'll let him cool down*, he thought to himself. *We'll talk this out when I get back*, and he drove off with Shelly. But it would be a while before they saw their son again.

Sody hid in the woods while his dad searched their property for him. Frustrated his dad wouldn't let him do what he wanted, his temper started to take over. Sometimes Sody had a raw, unrefined temper that flicked on like a light switch. He didn't like it, nor did he know how to control it. His family even started calling him Rumplestiltskin, a character from a fairytale that constantly loses his temper. "Rumplestiltskin, Rumplestiltskin," they would joke, and it always made him even more upset. He knew they were only teasing and trying to make light of the situation. Nonetheless, his temper had a mind of its own . . . just like Rumple.

After his parents left, he remained hidden, laying underneath the cover of a grove of young balsams just off the driveway. He figured his siblings would likely be going swimming again soon since it was another scorcher. Sody didn't intend to swim. He wanted to explore. Something deep inside him urged him to go out and see things with his own eyes. To find the truth for himself and not the truth that others told him. Yet, there was something else too. A feeling in the pit of his stomach, just a whisper, that said, *stay home, go swimming, be like the others.* He quickly quieted the whisper.

Keegan threw open the screen door of the camper and hopped down to the gravel drive. He made his way over to the clothesline where his swim trunks still hung from an earlier swim. Sody noticed it was still damp and heard Keegan groan.

"Uhhhh . . . I *hate* putting on wet swim trunks."

Sody had to agree. Maybe one other bad thing about summer was putting on wet swim trunks.

He watched from under the balsam trees as his siblings raced down to the lake, wet swimsuits and all. The whisper came back. *You're much better off going swimming, forget about seeing the other end of the lake. Go on your vision quest later.* But a louder murmur coaxed him to go on. *Grab your canteen and a compass. It's time to live, Sody.*

Slowly, he crept out from his hiding place, keeping an eye on the beach to make sure no one saw him. He sprinted to the camper, filled his metal canteen from the spring water they had collected in a large blue water container, and then sifted through his backpack searching for his compass. *What the heck . . . where is it?* He couldn't find it. It was missing. Gone.

"Oh well, I'll be fine," he reassured himself. But his stomach said otherwise. He wasn't planning on being gone more than a few hours, so it wouldn't be a big deal. Grabbing his pocket-knife from his tackle box, he tossed it in his pack and hopped back out of the camper. He had received the knife as a gift from an uncle the Christmas before. He treated it like his baby and brought it everywhere with him. A lot could be done with a little pocketknife; cut fishing line, make a marshmallow roasting stick, remove a splinter, perform an emergency tracheotomy (he had seen that in a movie). The knife was perhaps the small sense of security he needed that persuaded him to take it along.

Laughing and yelling could be heard coming from the beach. *They are having a ball*, he thought. It wasn't too late, there was still time to back out. Part of him wanted to slap on his wet swim trunks and cannonball off the dock. Sody battled himself, *one sign, if I get any bad sign I'll turn back. Just. One. Sign.* He snuck down to the end of the driveway, waiting for a warning, an omen, something. Five minutes went by, maybe ten. Nothing. So he kept on. With his canteen and pristine pocketknife stowed away into the depths of his school bag strapped over both shoulders—Sody kept on.

Washkish Road wound back and forth through the Chippewa National Forest. On the east side of Lake Napoleon, the trail was bordered on one side by spruce plantations and giant, native Norway Pines. The other side was a white cedar swamp that stretched for miles and miles, its undergrowth covered with thick moss and brambles and thickets that made it nearly impossible to see in.

Sody plodded along, holding onto both backpack straps and kicking rocks along the gravel trail. A sign never came, no warning that told him to turn around. It was kind of exciting breaking the rules, an adrenaline rush he had not yet experienced much before. He walked around the bend, singing a song his grandpa often played. The song that was playing when he had gone blueberry picking with his mom and sister.

I was a highwayman
Along the coach roads I did ride.

Down the road about a mile, he came across an old, tattered sign tacked onto a large poplar that read,

RINGLEADER ROAD

An arrow on the sign pointed down a trail. Underneath, someone had scrawled a short riddle.

WHAT YOU SEEK IS HERE, HIDDEN AND HARD.
FOR THOSE WHO FOLLOW, MOST WILL FAIL.
BUT THERE IS A REWARD, IF YOU DO GO FORWARD.

Sody stared at this for a while, pondering what it could mean. Ringleader Road wasn't much of a road, but rather a narrow trail that jutted off from the Washkish. It appeared to cut through the cedar swamp, but where it led he had no idea. He had never been down there. The cedar trees and spruce trees and alder brush were so close together down the trail they seemed to almost create a tunnel, with branches that formed some sort of natural arch six feet off the ground. Sody peered down the dark and eerie passage.

"What you seek is here, hidden and hard," he whispered aloud, "for those who follow . . . most will fail." It seemed dangerous, yet inviting, "But there is a reward, if you do go forward."

That's when Sody heard the crack of thunder overhead. He looked up to see an apocalyptic storm rolling in from the northeast. The sky turned an angry red and orange and black. Its coal-colored clouds carried with them rain and hail that could strike down at any moment. Sody looked up, horrified, his feet frozen in time, as blue and green lightning spider-webbed across the sky. The storm was alive and coming for him. He had been so focused on his new adventure and the woods and trails that he forgot to keep an eye on the weather. Now he only had two choices. He could dash into the cover of the unknown tunnel, down Ringleader Road, or hightail it back to the camper. The latter seemed smarter, perhaps safer, but the former was inviting and intriguing. It was as if the tunnel was trying to persuade him. He needed to decide fast.

Sody decided to head back down the Washkish where he came from to try and beat the storm, but it was too late. The sky opened up above him. A thick wall of rain glided towards him like an ancient ghost. He turned to face the other end of the Washkish only to see another wall, this one made of hailstones the size of ping pong balls. The two walls pressed in, suffocating his thoughts with their impending roar.

He leapt off the road, headfirst into the tunnel down Ringleader Road, just as the two walls clashed fiercely together.

WHOOSH!

Laying there, he peered back to see the rain and hail flooding towards the tunnel like a monsoon . . . and then the tunnel closed.

Thip. Like a thunder clap. . .

Just like that it shut. Barricaded by trees and branches and thickets. He didn't know it then, but he had crossed the barrier from the real world into the spirit world. His vision quest had just begun.

Darkness and silence enveloped him. Sody couldn't even see his outstretched hand. It was midnight black. Eerily quiet. But he escaped the storm, or rather, the trail saved him from it.

What is this, Sody thought to himself, *am I dreaming?*

"Hello, Sody," a peculiar voice came from the darkness, "we've been waiting for you."

"Who's been waiting for me? How do you know my name?" Sody was terrified at first but was quickly reassured. The voice was calming, like the one he'd been hearing in his head.

"We are the manidoog."

"The manidoog? Why did you save me . . . er, h . . . how did you save me?"

"You were in trouble, but your heart is in the right place. We help people who help themselves."

"Are you the ones who made up that riddle? The one on the sign?" inquired Sody, still laying on the mossy floor of the tunnel.

"We are not," echoed the voice, "perhaps that was someone who came before you."

"What is this place anyways? It would be nice if I could see something."

Far off down the tunnel a faint purple light flicked on. It started to spread towards Sody. Slowly, a dim purplish glow illuminated the passage lined by branches and brambles. The tunnel was not unlike any ordinary walking trail through the forest except the trees were wound tightly together and the branches above crisscrossed each other so thoroughly that one could not see through.

"This is the entrance to everything you've ever dreamed of, Sody. You will find that the path is rocky and uncertain, but you decided to come, so we the manidoog know you must be special. Most people don't come down this road. It's too difficult for them, or perhaps it is too unrealistic for them. They don't believe in themselves enough to give this route a chance. And of those who do venture this way, not all make it. It is demanding and scary and dare we say, risky."

"Why is it so scary and risky? What happens to those who don't make it?"

"We can't tell you that. Some things you must find out for yourself. After all, that's why you went on this journey today, isn't it?" the manidoog asked seriously. "You wanted to discover what it was like to do what you really want, to make your own decisions. So here is your chance, Sody. The gate is closed, now you must continue on. Enjoy your time here. And don't forget," they said, "ask and you shall receive."

Sody picked himself up off the soft ground. He felt lighter, stronger, and more awake than he'd ever been.

"Follow the tunnel, Sody, there is much to see."

Not seeing any other option, Sody began walking down the tunnel towards the source of the purple light. Why he felt so at home, he did not know. A gush of warmth and intrinsic power washed over his body and mind and soul. He felt free. Awake. Alive.

The fragrance from the spruce branches filled the fresh air of the passageway. Their piney scent so strong he stopped to take a deep breath, drinking the air. It smelled mesmerizing. A subtle breeze drifted through, cooling Sody's face and racing heart. His breathing slowed.

The farther he walked, the thinner the spruce and cedar walls became. The roof above began to separate, the branches no longer interlocking. Rays from the sun penetrated the once dark tunnel. Sody squinted. Up ahead the purple glow faded, and in the distance, hiding behind conifers and birches and poplars, was the lake glistening from the rays of the sun. He only had to get back to the lake. There he could regain his bearings.

He felt elated. He discovered a new world that he wasn't aware even existed. The entire forest looked alive and incredibly green. The sky a wondrous blue! And the dirt trail, dusty and dry and ancient. There were primroses and forget-me-nots hiding beneath the canopy of the forest and birds singing a summer hymn. *Yes, I really am alive, and isn't it something to truly feel alive.*

"Keep going, Sody. Plenty more lies ahead." The voice of the manidoog echoed once more through his heart and mind.

"Here I go!" said Sody.

And he took off. Like an antelope in open prairie, like wind in a sail, Sody dashed along the trail, jumping over logs that crisscrossed the path, jumping off boulders and jumping into his new found enjoyment of life. Today was his day and he must see what lay ahead. Time no longer mattered. He yearned to discover more.

CHAPTER 8

The Woods

Sody couldn't help but think about his family. He already missed them, and a sense of loneliness overcame him and welled in his eyes. Did they miss him too? Probably. How long had he been gone? Were his parents back yet? A powerful surge of guilt melted over him thinking about what he said to his dad before they left. *I'm a terrible son. And now I may never get to apologize.*

He noticed the trail getting narrower and narrower the farther he walked and the more he thought. The woods around him appeared to change. The bright green forest dimmed, and a large cloud blocked out the warmth of the sun. There came a low growl from behind him.

He whipped around only to see his family's chocolate lab standing in the middle of the trail. He let out an audible sigh of relief thinking it could have been something else. Something much more sinister.

"Mocha! How'd you find me?" Sody bent down and rubbed her head. "It's okay girl, it's just me. I'm scared too."

Mocha licked his face in glee. She had followed him down the Washkish and into the tunnel without him knowing. She was crafty like that.

The more he thought about the safety of home and his fear of the unknown, the darker the woods became. The two trudged on. Just above the tree line across the lake rested the sun, sinking slowly and carrying its light with it. Sody hadn't brought a flashlight. He never planned on being out so late. Oddly, though, it didn't feel like he had been out very long. It felt like an hour, or maybe two. The sun shouldn't be setting so early. Surely his parents were already looking for him though, or so he hoped. Strangely, it was beautiful being alone in the woods, but also petrifying.

As he looked ahead, he observed the thickets shaking and not long after a small black bear cub stumbled clumsily out into the open. Sody and Mocha watched it intently. It looked adorably innocent, sniffing the ground in search of something. Then it caught their scent and made a small squealing noise. Almost immediately, Sody heard a hearty growl coming from behind him.

"Mocha, shhh . . . it's okay." Sody said, trying to calm his dog.

He looked to his side and saw his chocolate lab sitting right next to him. Mocha wasn't the one that growled. They both looked back and saw an enormous black bear, standing on its two feet and baring its menacing teeth at them. A child eater, a shaggy one, a black brute! It was the cub's mother. A great sow! Her coat dark as coal and her eyes like small fiery suns. Sody's mind flashed to what his dad had said about bears being able to outrun most humans.

Woof! Woof! Mocha let out a deep, throaty bark Sody had never heard her utter before.

The bear dropped down to all fours, clacking its teeth and

grunting. The sound was enough to make his blood run cold. He stood in place, petrified.

CLACK CLACK CLACK CLACK!

Mocha's throaty bark turned into a whimper as the bear lumbered slowly toward them, knowing they had no way out. It was going to feast tonight. Suddenly, an idea popped into Sody's head. It was a stretch, but he tried it anyway.

"Manidoog . . . I . . . I need you. I need your help."

The bear inched closer, Sody and Mocha were too scared to move.

"You could run Sody. But the bear will probably catch you. What's in your pack?" It was the manidoog. They were still there!

Wonderful, Sody thought, *maybe there is a chance.*

"I have my canteen . . . and my knife! I forgot about my knife!"

"Perfect. Grab your knife. You can't run from this bear, it is too fast. You must attack it head on. Conquer it. Defeat it. And then forget about it. Take out your knife, Sody."

Sody fumbled through his pack and dug out the knife that was buried at the bottom. He flicked it open.

Click.

Its five-inch blade seemed all too small to do any real damage to the mammoth-sized creature. But he must try. Mocha cowered behind Sody. So much help *she* was!

The bear stopped abruptly ten yards short of them and stood back up on two legs. She towered above him. It was at least seven feet tall. She reached out her massive paws and scratched at a tall red pine. Her claws like arched daggers dug deeply into the bark. Wood chips and bark exploded from the tree. Sody could only think that he would be next.

Then the bear quit scratching and lumbered towards the boy and his dog once more. Sody recited the advice from the manidoog over and over in his head, attack it head on, conquer it, defeat it, and forget about it. It gave him courage that they believed in him. He had to kill the bear to save himself and his dog.

The bear closed in. Sody couldn't believe how something so big could also be so fast. Her fangs glistened in the glow of the rising moon and then her jaw snapped shut. Huffing, jaw popping.

CLACK!

Sody ducked just in time and the bear's fangs clamped shut on a pine branch above, snapping it off the tree. While the bear thrashed about attempting to get the branch out of its teeth, Sody saw his chance. He wheeled his blade, lunged awkwardly towards the bear, eyes shut, arms outstretched. . .

The knife sank through the flesh and into the heart of the bear with surprising ease. Sody opened his eyes. The bear stumbled backwards, part of the branch still sticking to her teeth. Her fiery eyes looked down upon Sody, showing defeat, then they went cold and shut.

Thump!

The ground rumbled as the great brute hit the forest floor. Fallen leaves and dirt sprang up and floated in mid-air, for just a second, illuminated from the light of the moon above, before falling back to the ground. And then the forest was silent except for the sound of Sody's heart beating out of his chest. Mocha sat on his feet, looking him in the eye as if to say, 'You saved me, Sody, and you saved yourself.'

He collapsed in a heap against the tree the bear had slashed. The fear exhausted him. It took all his energy. Then gradually, the purple glow came back to the dark woods and he finally relaxed a little. *Deep breaths*, he told himself, *deep breaths*. He recited a poem he had once heard in school over and over again in his head. A classic from Robert Frost called "Stopping by Woods on a Snowy Evening".

> *The woods are lovely, dark, and deep,*
> *But I have promises to keep,*
> *And miles to go before I sleep,*
> *And miles to go before I sleep.*

This calmed him. There was much he still had to do and much he yearned to see. No time for rest. Mocha licked his face. She agreed. No time for rest.

"Okay, okay I'll get up. But next time you need to be a little bit more helpful, alright?"

Mocha let out a soft yip. *Okay Sody.*

Sody gathered himself and stood up to walk over to the bear. He made his peace with the animal and trotted back down the trail followed by his loyal companion. It was an Ojibwe ritual to make peace with any animal that is sacrificed for the greater good. The woods, although dark, regained their beauty after the attack. Things revealed themselves to him that he never really noticed before, at least not in a long time. He admired the uniqueness of the craters on the moon. The truth that it reflected off the surface of the lake. Somewhere, on the far end of the lake, an owl hooted its nightly tune.

Hoo-hoo. Hoo-hoo.

His hair pricked up on the back of his neck. The sound so ghostly, and earthly and wonderful.

Ringleader Road seemed to be illuminated by some sort of clairvoyance. Probably it was just the slant of the moon, but the trail appeared a touch brighter than the rest of the woods.

"One sees clearly only with the heart, Sody," the manidoog said, startling him.

Can they read my thoughts? Creepy. He kept on.

The boy and his dog trudged deeper into the woods. Woods enchanted with voices who called themselves the manidoog and strange lights that calmed the soul and rogue bears and yes . . . woods enchanted with hope and strength and despair. *How can the manidoog communicate with me? What are the strange lights? And the bear . . . the honeyeater, why did she attack me? Maybe she thought I was a threat to her kin.* His mind raced with questions that had no clear answers. He kept on. He needed to figure out what it all meant. Why was he here? And would he ever be able to return home from this mysterious, otherly world.

The more he desired to get through the woods, the brighter the trail became. What was once a dark night became light with help from the moon. Then soon enough it turned to dawn. The darkness melted away to make room for the sun, to make room for the light.

The voices spoke to him again. The manidoog.

"In this place, the sun doesn't set when it's supposed to set . . . and the moon doesn't rise when it's supposed to rise. The darkness can come anytime, and so can the light. There may be storms that come when you least expect them, and creatures that try to stop you from continuing on the road you are on. But just as there are storms and unwelcoming beasts, so there is sunshine and helping hands. It is up to you who wins. Our advice to you, since you've made it this far, is to keep going. Give it a shot. Do you have any other option?"

The manidoog had a way of flittering into his brain whenever he questioned what lay ahead.

"Give what a shot?" replied Sody with curiosity.

"Why, your dreams of course."

"Oh . . . But my dreams are large and plentiful. What if I can't live them out? What if I fail? In school they don't teach us to follow dreams. They teach us how to pass tests and they tell us to go to college. One of my teachers even told us specifically *not* to follow our dreams because they aren't always realistic."

"That is no teacher!" boomed the manidoog, "that is a taker."

Sody shuddered at the change in tone. "A . . . a taker?"

"Someone who takes your dreams. Takes your courage and your willpower. Those kinds of people are gutless and fearful. Takers take because they couldn't reach their own goals, so they don't want others to pursue theirs. They are cynical and cowardly. Don't let them take your purpose, Sody."

"I won't," said Sody with such certainty that it must be true. "I'll never let them take from me or from anyone else. I want to help others."

"That is great. That's the spirit, but first you must help yourself."

"I will." He furrowed his brow in a look of fortitude. "I'll help myself," he concluded.

His heart surged. His soul swelled. He had never felt so full of purpose. *If people didn't follow their dreams*, he thought, *how could they get the most out of life? How could anyone do what they really wanted - what they were meant to do, if all they ever did was settle, if they always let the takers win?*

Sody developed an inner dialogue with the manidoog. It was as if an older, wiser version of himself was giving him advice. They were connected yet separate at the same time. This troubled him. *Surely, I mustn't tell anyone for they will think I am crazy,* he thought to himself. And most people absolutely would. But maybe he wasn't so crazy, maybe *he* was the sane one. The one who thought he could change the world. Maybe the crazy ones were the ones who *didn't* think like him, who thought that a person can only do so much and only so much one person can be.

The woods came to life with the rising of the sun. Mocha ran around chasing after a red squirrel. Birds filled the air with songs of a new day.

Chicka-dee-dee-dee-dee.

Twit-twoo twit-twooo.

And Sody kept on. Stick-to-it-iveness. He recalled the made-up word a teacher had once told him. She wasn't a taker, but a real teacher, someone who cared. Stick-to-it-iveness. It meant striving for something; an idea, a goal, a passion, no matter what obstacles hinder the plan. And so, he decided he would. He would stick to his journey. As with anything, resilience is key, especially when it comes to chasing dreams.

Ringleader Road curled down a shallow ridge to the lake. The coniferous forest now blended with birches and towering poplars. A breeze rustled through the leaves, creating a thousand-and-one shades of green that fused with the blues of the sky and the lake to create a palate of summer. It was dazzling. Breathtaking right down to the bone. Sody bounded down the trail with Mocha in close pursuit. As they rounded the final bend to the lake, they saw two boys at the shore skipping rocks.

"Hey! Hey guys!" he shouted while running down to the lake.

The two figures quit skipping rocks and turned to see Sody and Mocha barreling towards them.

He soon recognized them.

"Chester! Dakota!" yipped Sody in a high voice, "What are you guys doing here?"

"We came to help you. You didn't really believe we would let you do this all alone, did you?" Chester exclaimed.

"He's right, Sodes." Dakota chimed in. "Whenever you need us, we'll be there. Maybe not always in person, but in spirit."

"You guys really are a sight for sore eyes." Sody raised his arms above his head and tried to catch his breath. "You wouldn't believe the things that have happened to me."

All three of them sat down next to the shoreline while Sody filled them in on the events that transpired since starting down Ringleader Road.

"Well done, Sody," echoed the voices of the manidoog. "You have found your friends. You will need them on your journey, just like they may need you on theirs someday."

Sody peeked at Chester, then turned to Dakota. "Did you guys hear that?"

"Hear what?" said Chester confused.

"Nothing. Never mind. Must have just been the wind."

Chester and Dakota looked puzzled, both scrunching their foreheads simultaneously.

Sody stood up and faced the lake. "Maybe we should keep going. There is much still to see." He found himself talking just like the manidoog. *Odd. How very curious,* he thought.

"Sounds good to me. What way should we go?" Chester asked Sody. He pointed over his shoulder. "Heading south would be the quickest way back to your place."

Sody pondered this for a moment. He set his hands on his hips in contemplation. "I suppose it would be, but I'm not going back there. Not yet. There is something I need to discover on the far end of the lake. I've never been there before. I don't think many people have. Would you guys care to join me?"

He silently prayed they would agree to join him.

"Let's do this," responded Dakota quickly. He was always up for adventure, especially when he had Sody by his side. Sody could always count on him. Chester, on the other hand, was a bit more of a realist.

Chester spoke up, "Uhhh . . . that's a long ways. And your parents . . . what about them? Won't they be wondering where you are?" He started rambling. He was always the conscience of the group. "We could get lost . . . but you know . . . I'm always up for an adventure. I'm in."

Sody knew he could always count on Chester too. He felt very fortunate to have such loyal friends. If not for them he wasn't so sure where or who he would be. They shook hands. Another deal. A handshake was as good as writing in stone. A binding, unspoken agreement among friends, deeply rooted in faith and loyalty. An unbreakable bond. They kept on.

CHAPTER 9
The Pit

The sun's rays beat down hotly on the earth, yet the air felt thin, the oppressive humidity of a Minnesota summer all but gone. Not a cloud appeared in the bluebird sky. Nor a breeze while they walked through woods enchanted. Ringleader Road widened just enough for the three boys to walk side-by-side. A day of days. A midsummer adventure.

Mocha trotted innocently out ahead, tongue lolling out to the side of her mouth in utter enjoyment. She tilted her nose up to sniff the air and took in the perfume of an uncharted forest. So pure. So primal. So genuine. She peeked back over her shoulder.

Woo-woof!

Must be going the right way.

The Norway pines bordering the trail pierced the sky like Jack's beanstalk, reaching up to faraway lands in the wild blue yonder. They were colossal, herculean wonders of the wild forest. Probably they'd been there since the first conscious thought. First as seedlings, young, and fragile. And now as giants, seasoned, and wise.

Chester broke the silence, "This place is gorgeous."

"And wild," said Dakota.

"It really is. I wish everyone could see this place. I wonder why we haven't seen anyone else on this trail. It's beautiful," concluded Sody.

"Maybe 'cause there's bears!" joked Chester. All three chuckled quietly.

"You're probably right." Sody said soberly, thinking of his bear attack. He gazed down at his feet and kicked a small rock off the path.

"Sorry, Sodes. I didn't mean to bring that up," said Chester.

"It's okay, you guys are here now. It's safer. I don't think a bear would attack us three anyway. We are kings of the forest! Slayers of beasts!"

"You're right. . ." Dakota said with an air of dignity, "far better off together than separate. There is nothing that can stop us."

Together, the three boys walked through the forest that surrounded Lake Napoleon. The magic of summer glimmered in every lazy leaf and wrinkly wave out on the lake. Back at the camper, however, the rest of the Fairbanks were a wreck. Sody's parents didn't sleep a wink the night he didn't return home. Their child was gone. Where could he be? On another reckless adventure? Most likely. But why hadn't he come back? And to leave without telling his siblings a word. Nothing. Their son had gone mad! That was it, he was mad. Or worse, lost in the forest full of known and unknown dangers. The unexplained. The unexplored. Sody, gone missing. Send out the search party! This calls for a rescue mission! This boy needs saving!

As the sun slowly started its descent, the three boys approached a sharp rise in the trail. It happened to be that still time of day when the high noon buzzing of cicadas had quit, and the evening mosquito ambush had yet to begin. No crows cawing. No loons uh-loooing. But a light, steady breeze started from the south. Just enough to tickle the leaves. The woods were nearly silent. Just nearly.

"Last one to the top has to carry my backpack!" yelled Sody, and with that he took off running up the hill.

Chester lunged helplessly at his heels but missed. "Cheater!"

"Guys, my shoe's untied!" cried Dakota, clambering up after them. Soon they were all up at the top.

"Thanks for the heads-up, losers. I think Chester should ha. . ." Dakota trailed off.

They all looked down the hill. Before them lay an enormous gravel pit bordered on either side by a dense cedar swamp full of brambles and thickets and heaven knows what else.

Sody scanned and scanned with a hand to his brow. "I can't see the lake anymore."

"Where *are* we?"

"My dad never said anything about a gravel pit. . . . I guess he never said much at all about the other places around the lake. Or even anything about this trail we've been following."

"Why don't you think he told you any of that? Don't you think that's a little weird?" asked Chester, studying Sody. "I mean, he must know about this. Dads know everything."

"Maybe he didn't want you coming back here is all. Maybe he thought you'd want to come explore this," added Dakota.

"Little late for that don't you think, Dakota?" said Sody. They chuckled unconvincingly, standing right on the edge of a steep bank above the pit.

The gravel pit was massive. A hundred yards long and another hundred wide. At least. From where they were standing it was a twenty-foot drop to the bottom, and in the middle of the pit, scattered like dragon's teeth, were tall mounds of what appeared to be large, sandy, pointed domes. Sody grabbed a large branch from the ground and walked right to the edge of the pit. The toes of his shoes crept out over the bank as he gazed down to the bottom.

"What are you doing Sodes? Are you crazy?" asked Chester in disbelief.

He peered back at his two friends, who stared helplessly at him with jaws agape. "Watch this."

Sody bent down and jabbed the long branch into the sand of the embankment. Then he walked off the edge of the bank.

"Sody!" Dakota and Chester screamed, their voices echoing across the gravel pit. They scurried to the edge to witness their best friend fall to his most certain death.

"Woohoooo!" Sody was sliding down the sandy cliff with his feet on the branch. Not falling, but sliding. He appeared to be riding a big wave of sand all the way to the bottom. The Duke Kahanamoku of gravel pit surfing!

"Made it!"

Chester and Dakota stood watching, eyes wide, and shook their heads in disbelief when he somehow made it to the bottom unscathed.

"You're crazy!" shouted Chester from the top.

"Out of your mind!" added Dakota, "but also, genius! That was awesome."

Chester and Dakota scanned the area to find an easier path down to the bottom. One that didn't involve surfing sand waves.

"I can't believe you just did that. I wish we had it on video.

You would be famous. I can see it now," Chester said with hands outstretched, making an invisible headline, "Thirteen-year-old boy surfs twenty-foot wave of sand!"

"And does it with his shirt on," finished Dakota.

"You guys are hilarious. Should have given it a try. You only live once," shouted Sody from the bottom of the pit.

"Yeah, and I'd like to live till I'm at least *fifteen*," said Chester in a higher voice than usual.

The two boys eventually found their way to the base of the sand pit using a much gentler slope. Sand, sand everywhere, like a desert in the middle of the woods. The domes stuck out of the sand like gigantic shark fins, forty yards away, looming taller than any of the three boys. They were impressive and intimidating and peculiar.

Dakota walked carefully towards the domes. He sized them up with uncertainty. "What the heck *are* those things. . . ?"

"Only one way to find out." Sody gripped the branch above his head and followed Dakota. "You know . . . in case we need it for something," he said to the questioning gazes of his two friends.

Onward they trudged through soft sand.

Walking up to the first micro-pyramid, they noticed it was made of hardened sand with thousands of tiny holes dotting its unearthly surface.

"I've never seen anything like it," Chester said. "Any idea on what this is guys?" It wasn't often Chester didn't know the facts about something. He was a bit of a genius. And wouldn't it have been nice if he was genius enough to know what the mounds were?

"Huh. . ." trailed Sody, tightening his grip on the branch. Then he swung it two-handed.

WACK!

Not only was it a surfboard but a baseball bat too! Nothing happened. The sand, incredibly hardened, created a shock from the connection of the stick and the mound sending vibrations up Sody's arm, rattling the bones in his forearms.

They walked farther among the pyramids of sand that looked like dragon's teeth. Smack dab in the center of all the others, there appeared to be a freshly built mound.

Sody wound up like a Major League Baseball player, wielding his Swiss Army branch.

WAAACK!

Earlier, he imitated surfing legend Duke Kahanamoku and now he was Babe Ruth! The branch sliced through the center of the mound like a katana through a watermelon, but instead of seeds flying everywhere, it was ants. By the millions. Chester and Dakota stood by, helplessly watching the amazingly terrible grand slam their friend just crushed.

"RUNNN!" Chester hollered.

"Home Run?" Sody turned around with a smile as big as the Rio Grande.

"No . . . RUN!!!" yelled Dakota and took off, kicking up sand and dust and ants. So long, suckers!

In the explosion of sand from his hit, Sody hadn't yet seen the millions of tiny arthropods scurrying beneath him. By the time he finally realized he had crushed a mountainous anthill, they were crawling up his legs. He batted them away with his branch, but they kept coming and coming and coming. The ground appeared to be moving and spreading like a black plague. Finally, Sody chased after his buddies, who were spitting up a cloud of dust on their way to the other end of the gravel pit. *So much for helping each other out*, Sody thought.

I see how it is, you smash one anthill and suddenly it's every-
one for themselves.

If not for the biggest blunder in Major League Antball history, Sody and Dakota and Chester might have seen what lay past
all of the giant ant hills. They may have skirted past it, silently
and safely, but when you are running from a hoard of biting
ants, you don't watch your step.

After finally making it out of the maze of dragon's teeth,
Sody looked around. He was sure Dakota and Chester would
be waiting for him atop the gravel pit, standing safely above the
sea of ants, yet there they were, not twenty feet away.

"Guys, what are you doing?" questioned Sody. "We gotta
get to the top of the pit now, before all these ants eat us alive!"

"Don't take another step," blurted Dakota.

Too late. Sody took a step towards them and felt his foot
sink oddly below the surface of the sand. He fought frantically
to lift it back out but it proved impossible. He eventually realized his friends were already knee deep in the stuff.

"Quicksand," said Chester precisely.

"Thanks, Chester, for clarifying." Sody shot back. "This is it.
We're doomed. We are going to get eaten by ants and nobody
will ever find our bodies. I could think of a hundred better ways
to go than this."

Dakota spoke up. He looked extraordinarily calm. "We lived
good lives, boys. In the olden days this was like the regular age
for dying I'm pretty sure."

"Not quite," added Chester lifting his hand and pointing to
the sky with his index finger. "The average age of mortality was
closer to thirty, not thirteen."

"Alright, enough you two!" interrupted Sody. "Really, Chester?
You choose now to spit facts at us? Would have been nice if you

had known that those were anthills back there. Then maybe we wouldn't be in this mess right now."

"Well, if you wouldn't have been swinging at them like a drunken Babe Ruth, we would be okay too."

Sody blushed and admitted, "That's a dang good point."

The ants kept coming, their tiny legs pitter-pattering back and forth across the sand as swift as they could. Time was quickly running out. Sody would be eaten first. The ants closed in on him. He accepted that his friends would have to watch him get devoured by the tiny red-black army. What a torturous and gruesome way to go.

Dakota and Chester sunk to their waists in the sand. Sody to his knees. The sand, oppressively hot, scorched their exposed skin. Their morale very quickly disappeared, and a deep, dark, helpless feeling set in. Hopelessness. It was something far worse than fear.

Now would be a nice time for mirages of innocent sandy beaches, or a waterfall, or a pretty girl, Sody thought, something to take the edge off the impending grisly deaths they all faced.

"Well boys, it was nice knowing yuh." The ants reached Sody's knees. He still had the branch and he batted them away by the hundreds. It was like trying to sweep a sandbox. Always more behind the ones getting swatted away. They kept coming and coming and coming. From all sides now. He felt them crawling up his legs. Thousands of them. Some bit. Some did not. Game over. . .

WOO-WOOF!

They quickly turned their heads to see Mocha careening down the bank of the gravel pit, her muscles rippling beneath the Hershey brown coat that glistened in the sun. She was on a mission. The ants were up to Sody's neck now. Stinging and biting everywhere. He reached the branch out to his chocolate lab. She grabbed it with her mouth and sunk her large feet into the sand. *Oh no*, Sody thought, *she's going to sink too.* But she merely planted her feet for a base. The stubby, powerful lab tugged and pulled and tugged and pulled with all her might, slowly backing up and gradually pulling Sody out of his pit of despair. He held on for dear life despite the intense pain of every ant bite. Finally, Mocha pulled him out and he collapsed in a heap next to the quicksand. Rolling over and over on the ground and shucking the ants from his arms and face and body he finally rid himself of the tiny devilish foes.

The ants now closed in on Chester and Dakota, who were nearly chest deep in the sand. For some reason the ants stayed away from Mocha, avoided her like there was some hidden force-field around her. A spectacle Sody could not believe. He shuffled his way closer to his friends, careful not to fall back into the quicksand. Bending low, he reached the branch out towards Chester who was just barely able to wrap his hands around the end of it. Sody heaved hard to tug him out but barely budged him. Too much sand swallowed his comrade.

"Come on Sodes . . . you gotta save me buddy." Chester sounded desperate. His eyes bulged with fear.

Dakota looked on helplessly. Speechless.

Sody kept tugging. Mocha set up behind him and clamped onto the waistband of his shorts with her teeth and tugged on Sody and Sody tugged on Chester and slowly they worked him loose from the grips of the greedy sediment.

One more to go.

They repeated the process with Dakota. Sody and Chester and Mocha looked like a mini conga line working their way over to their sinking comrade. From a bird's eye view it must have appeared that they were performing a choreographed dance which would have been quite an impressive one if that's what it was. It's much easier to dance when you literally have ants in your pants.

Finally, with one large, fateful tug and flurry of grunts, Dakota was freed. The ants, however, were not finished with them. Relentless little terrors they were. The boys scrambled to their feet and wheeled up the bank of the pit in a crazed pandemonium. Mocha sat at the top waiting for them. She licked Sody's hand. They all watched as the ants slowly moved up the slope like a rising tide. As the ants neared the top they slowed, then stopped all at once. And as quickly and menacingly as they came, they receded silently back to their home, or half of a home, thanks to Sody.

"Phew, talk about a close call," sighed Sody, with his hands on his hips.

"You're telling me."

Chester straightened up and brushed the dirt off his clothes. He inspected the countless bites that now covered his body, knowing it could have been much worse. "Thank heavens for that dog of yours, Sody. We would have been dinner for all those ants. I couldn't believe how many there were. That was creepy."

He exhaled deeply, finally regaining his breath. "I hope none of us ever have to go through anything like that a second time."

The manidoog had been watching them all along. They spoke to Sody.

"You see, Sody, sometimes the least expected help will come when you need it most. Keep on the path. You are going the right way. And enjoy the company of your friends, they won't always be there. The woods are lovely, aren't they Sody? But scary too. Goodbye for now, we bid you adieu."

Sody eyed Chester and Dakota. It was evident they hadn't heard the manidoog so he kept it to himself. He didn't want them thinking he was losing his mind.

They decided there was no point in turning back for home anymore. Dealing with quicksand and ants another time just did not sound appealing. And the manidoog told Sody that they were heading the right way. *The right way for what?* That was something they'd have to find out for themselves.

CHAPTER 10

The Abandoned Cabin

Leaving the gravel pit far behind, Sody and his two friends made their way back to Ringleader Road, laughing and gawking at the beautiful scenery around them.

Up ahead they came upon a fork in the road. One path trailed off to the west and the other went straight. Chester stopped at the fork and looked off to the horizon. "The sun's starting to set," he warned. "We need to seek some sort of refuge for the night, guys. Which way are you thinking?"

"I say we go left at the fork. That way should take us back to the lake. Maybe there will be a spot we can build a makeshift shelter or something," insisted Sody.

Dakota agreed. "Sodes is right. Let's try to make it back to the lake. If nothing else, we'll have a nice view and will be able to grasp our bearings again. It's kind of spooky being surrounded by woods at night."

"That sounds like a good idea to me." Chester was all about good ideas.

Mocha plodded up ahead. She must have been eavesdropping on the conversation because she ventured down the left side of the fork ahead of them, leading the way. The trail narrowed as the trees choked in ever so tightly. It was obvious from the start this part of the trail had rarely been taken, at least not recently.

It was near nightfall when the band of brothers and their trusty lab stumbled down the narrow lane which led them to an ancient, abandoned cabin. Lake Napoleon could be seen through the trees, its water dead still, no whisper of wind, so it reflected the backdrop of woods perfectly as the sun sank below the pines in front of them.

The cabin sat perched on a birch knoll overlooking the lake. Its windows had since been boarded up. *Why?* They hadn't the slightest idea. It was a dainty little cabin, with faded dark red wood siding and moss growing in patches on the green shingled roof. A large stone chimney stood unsteadily on the forest side of the cabin, crumbling from the wear of weather and time. An eerie silence hung in the air, as if the mouth of the woods had been sewn shut to hide an everlasting secret.

Mocha eyed the cabin wearily, growling softly.

"Shhhh . . . It's okay girl." Sody tried calming her, although he too felt uncertain about the cabin. He studied the concerned looks on the faces of his friends. "Well guys, it's almost dark. This is our only option right now."

Chester backed into Dakota who stood directly behind him. "No way I'm going in there. Absolutely not. You couldn't pay me to sleep in that thing." He was rambling again. "There's probably dead people in there, or worse, ghosts!"

Dakota grabbed Chester's shoulders firmly and set him aside. He was unusually strong for his size. "Oh, don't be a bunch of wimps. It's just an old cabin. I bet you ten bucks there's a nice comfy set of bunk beds in there with our names on them. And stock full of firewood *right* next to the fireplace."

Sody sighed. "Only one way to find out I guess."

Dakota skipped fearlessly to the front door of the cabin. He swung open the screen door and it flew off the hinges and onto the ground in a heap.

"That's promising," mumbled Chester from the background. "The entire cabin is probably going to fall apart on us."

"If that doesn't kill us it'll be the mold or asbestos," Dakota said sarcastically, although he hadn't the slightest clue what asbestos was. He saw it on a commercial once and it sounded dangerous.

Chester rolled his eyes so hard he got a glimpse of his brain.

The entry door did not budge on the first try or the second, nor would the handle turn.

"Locked," said Chester.

"I was hoping it would be." Dakota fumbled around in his pants pocket and pulled out what appeared to be a pair of tools stolen from a dentist's office. "Got these for Christmas last year from my uncle Rick. Watch this."

He inserted two ends into the keyhole of the door handle and twisted them counterclockwise.

Click.

He turned to face his buddies who looked on, dumb-founded. Smiling, he turned the knob on the door and opened it up into the dark cabin. Fumbling through his pocket once more, he pulled out a small Zippo lighter. Flicking the wheel by snapping his fingers against it, the lighter flared up, emitting a small flame just bright enough to illuminate the inside of the small space.

The cabin opened up to one large room, loosely divided by furnishings into separate spaces for the kitchen, dining area, and living room. Old, dust covered pans were left next to the sink to dry. It appeared no one had been there in years. They must be dry by now! Three wooden chairs surrounded the tiny dinner table, the fourth was laying on its back. And in front of the fireplace sat a large, mustard yellow L-shaped couch. Cobwebs dotted the nooks and crannies of nearly everything in the room. And up on the chimney, above the mantle, hung a large woodburning of an old Native chief. The name 'Busticogan' was inscribed at the bottom of the portrait. Sody thought he had heard his grandpa say that name before.

Dakota grabbed an old newspaper off the table that dated back to 1998 and walked over to the fireplace. The headline read "Lost and Found" and displayed a picture of a young boy being pulled out of a cave. He shrugged and tossed it in the fireplace, then stacked kindling on top of it in a log cabin formation. Using his lighter, he lit the paper, and flames quickly spread to the little logs and illuminated the entire cabin with a yellow-orange light that flickered eerily off the walls, creating creepy shadows across the room and made the woodburning portrait above the fireplace come to life.

Sody peered around the cabin with hands on his hips. He moved to the center of the space and turned to face his friends. "Wish we had a little more light . . . but this will have to do. Did you guys bring anything to eat? I'm starving. And that can of beans sitting next to the stove is at least five years expired."

Chester, who stood in the kitchen area, emptied the contents of his bag on the ancient wooden table. Fruit roll-ups, rice crispy treats and a plastic bag jammed full with his mom's homemade brownies spilled out like a cracked-open piñata.

Dakota grabbed a fruit roll-up. "Jackpot."

"Your mom always has the hookups Chester. She knows exactly what we like," said Sody with a mouthful of rice crispy bar.

Dakota nodded his head in agreement. His mouth full of fruit roll-up.

Chester responded for Dakota. "She really does. She wanted to throw in some apples and bananas, but I told her we wouldn't eat them anyway."

"That's probably true. We have all the fruit we need in these fruit roll-ups!"

Chester and Dakota chuckled at this while chewing on their sugary strands of "fruit".

"Mocha, come here girl," beckoned Sody, "sit." She sat. "Good girl, now shake." Mocha lifted her paw up to Sody's hand and shook it gently.

"Good job, now here's a treat." He tossed her the other half of his rice crispy bar, which she gladly chomped and swallowed in a single bite.

It had been an exhausting day for them all and wasn't it nice to finally relax a little. The fire crackled quietly, their tummies were full, and the mustard yellow couch was as soft as a cloud.

Sody yawned.

Dakota eyed him mischievously. "Hey, no sleeping Sodes. We got ghost stories to tell," he said with a low, menacing voice.

"Relaaax, I wasn't going to sleep. Just a little tired is all. I mean, we did have quite a day battling those ants and that quicksand."

"You aren't kidding. A day of days. A fight of fights! And we came out with our lives!" Chester used his best motivational speech voice, something he was rather good at. "Today shall go down in history as the day the three musketeers battled an insurmountable army of ants. The three who banded together to withstand the clench of the earth's mighty grasp!"

Chester, only thirteen, had the vocabulary of a twenty-something-year-old by the time he turned six.

"You should write that down somewhere, Chester. An army general might want to use that speech in the future . . . or a president or tyrant," murmured Sody.

"Alright guys, who's ready for some ghost stories?" Dakota loved his ghost stories. More than anything he probably just enjoyed seeing people scared. He even scared himself sometimes. That was just the kind of person Dakota was. He craved anything that got his adrenaline rushing. All three boys enjoyed scary stories, but Dakota proved to always be a little more daring. A bit more wild.

The three scooted the couch closer to the fire. It might have been a hot summer night, but something about ghost stories wrapped one in a blanket of frost. Sody could attest to this.

Outside, no moon rose to light the night. The landscape was wrapped tight in a shroud of blackness and the only light escaping, like tiny pin holes in a black curtain, were the ever-distant stars. Even the light from the fire inside the cabin could not escape the boarded-up windows. All was quiet. All was still, except for the souls inside the shack.

Dakota reached between the cushion and arm of the couch looking for a lever to recline the seat back. Instead, he pulled out a small book. A paperback. The pages and cover were worn and cracked from overuse. On the front was a picture of a buried head of an old man with an emaciated face and a pipe in his mouth. He smiled, the man, with teeth bared and the pipe dangling from his rotted teeth. The whole picture black and white. In the background behind the man loomed a full moon over a graveyard.

"What the heck is that. . ." Sody's blood ran cold.

Dakota's hands shook unsteadily. "I . . . I don't know. It was in the couch. Between the cushions. It's not mine. I didn't bring it."

Chester's eyes looked like they might pop out of his head at any moment. "That's so creepy," he whispered almost inaudibly. "Don't open that. Whatever you do, don't."

"It's probably an old spell book from a witch or something." Chester glanced at Dakota, then at Sody. "I'm serious. Those things are real ya know."

Dakota opened the book. Of course he did. Why wouldn't he? Of the three, he was the only one who would have opened it. Chester and Sody would have tossed it in the fire and watched the pages of whatever was inside vanish into millions of tiny ashes and sparks. The words and pictures could have died, never to be seen or spoken again, except Dakota had been the one to find the book.

"Close that! Dakota, I'm serious," begged Sody. "Come on, man." He could feel fear wrapping its cold fingers around him. Soon it would envelop him.

"It's completely harmless you guys," said Dakota. "It looks like it's just a collection of old stories is all. Nothing to get all worked up about."

Mocha, who lay alert on the edge of the couch, whimpered softly and moved over to sit in front of Sody.

"See, even the dog doesn't want you to open it."

But it was too late.

"Aha, this looks like a good one. . . *Creature* by Jared Leberman." Dakota cleared his throat. Chester stoked up the fire knowing he couldn't stop Dakota from reading the story. Not without making him mad. Sody patted the back of Mocha's neck.

The Native chief above the mantle seemed to move slightly with each flicker of flame. Sody gazed up at the portrait of Busticogan. *Is he trying to tell me something?* He felt a connection to the chief but could not reason why. Outside, nothing stirred. The woods were waiting, listening. . .

Dakota began reading aloud the handwritten story scrawled into the book.

> "It was a quiet night and most of the town was asleep. Everyone except for two brothers, Tom and Louis Ostendorf. Tom was sixteen and Louis thirteen. It was the middle of October and the temperature showed it—the thermometer read thirty-eight degrees. The wind breezed through the trees, knocking free most of the remaining orange, yellow and red leaves and kicked them across the road."

Dakota eyed his two friends. Then continued.

> "Although it was a school night, the two brothers were out late driving around because Tom was excited that he recently got his driver's license.
> *We won't be gone long.* He had said to his mother before the two left. But Tom couldn't have been more wrong.
> After driving around town for some time, Tom decided to drive to the cemetery to scare his younger brother. He parked right outside the entrance. The full moon glistened upon every tombstone and cross. And a light fog had descended

upon the graves. Tom could see the scared look on his younger brother's face.

'What do you think? Should we go in there? I say we should rob some graves!' Tom joked.

Louis wanted to seem brave in front of Tom.

'Let's go in.' He said calmly.

So, Tom slowly pulled the car into the grave-yard. The road made a large loop through the cemetery and back out to the highway. It was sided by tombstones and a few looming elm trees."

Chester and Sody inched closer to the fire.

"Finally, they parked the car. There was a small lake on the backside of the graveyard, not much larger than a pond. Cemetery Lake it was called. The moon reflected off of its surface.

'Legend has it that the lake is stained with blood from all the people buried up here.' Tom said.

Louis went pale as a ghost.

'It's probably just a made-up story though,' Tom consoled his younger brother.

He put the car in drive and slowly made his way down the loop, driving past all the tombstones before circling back out to the highway."

Dakota cleared his throat. The fire was slowly dying down so that shadows stretched across the floor and the walls. Everything in the cabin became a whole lot spookier.

He continued reading.

"On their way back home, they came to a spot where a field was alongside the road. It was mostly barren except for the fog and the trees far off in the distance.

'Stop!' Louis yelled. 'Stop the car, I think I saw something!'

Tom slammed on the brakes. Then opened up his door.

'What are you doing?' Louis said.

Tom had already closed the car door and hopped over the ditch into the field. He went out about fifty yards but didn't see anything. Not a soul. However, when he turned around to head back to the car, he saw it. A tall figure standing between him and the car. It crept slowly towards him.

'H-hello. Can I help you? What are you doing out here?' said Tom.

No answer.

Slowly the figure became more and more visible. And less and less humanlike. It was wretched. The Creature. Whatever it was."

Dakota's storytelling voice sped up and grew more solemn.

"Tom yelled at the figure to stop, but it kept coming closer. He lost the ability to move. He was frightened beyond belief. His feet quit working. The creature's face was falling off grotesquely. He watched in horror as its jaw appeared between holes in the skin. Its eyes were large and steel blue with teeth sharp as fangs. All of them.

From the car, Louis heard screaming coming from the field but couldn't see because of the thick blanket of fog. They didn't last long, the screams. And before long a figure made its way across the field back to the car. The door opened up.

'Phew,' exclaimed Louis, 'I thought you might never come back.'

But when he turned to his brother he came face to face with the creature."

"AHHH!" Dakota screamed, sending, Sody and Chester jumping back into their seats.

Sody stared blankly into the fire. Eyes wide. It wasn't so much this particular story that frightened him, but the fact that it reminded him of the story his grandfather had told him just a few weeks prior. The story of the spirit of the north wind. He hadn't thought about that story in a while. In fact, he had nearly forgotten about it altogether until now. That's the thing about fear, it almost never loses its grip. It hangs on by the tiniest thread until it sees an opportunity to grab a handful and pull you further down.

Sody felt dread slowly begin to take over him. It was back, the spirit and its sinister presence. He knew he should rid the thought of it from his head. That the spirits of the north wind aren't real. That they were just a figment of imagination. The spirit, however, was also so much more. A beast so hungry and evil and quiet. It came unannounced. It needed no welcome. It needed just one thing. A drop of fear, or distress. Yes, it could feed on that and Sody knew it firsthand.

His friends could see the look on his face, and both Dakota and Chester struggled to see what bothered Sody so badly. If he had troubles, Sody never let it show. They didn't know he had any or *could* have any. He always seemed to be confidence personified. Nothing ever chinked his armor. Or so they thought. Now Sody's mind had become infested with thoughts of the spirit of the north wind. An unsolicited obsession.

Dakota slapped the book shut, startling both Chester and Sody. "Well, I suppose that's enough hocus pocus for now, huh?"

Sody kept his blank gaze on the dying fire. His face had turned pale. "Yeah . . . that's enough for now. Chester, wanna toss another log on the fire?"

Chester searched around the fireplace a bit more frantically than he cared to admit. "Uhmm . . . well I would, but . . . that's it." All eyes scanned the area for more wood.

"What do you mean that's it?" asked Sody.

Chester motioned to the remnants of the firewood next to the chimney. What used to be a pile of wood now contained only scraps of bark and tiny splinters of kindling. "We've used it all up. It's gone. It all went bye-bye."

"I'm kind of tired anyways," yawned Dakota. "Wouldn't mind hitting the sack and catching some Z's." He laid his head back on the arm of the couch and folded his hands behind himself nonchalantly. It didn't appear the story had shaken him at all. He was the definition of chill. Sody envied him. He used to be like that. He used to be strong minded, but not anymore. Something changed in him and he loathed it. Loathed the new him. It suffocated him.

"I spose . . . but still, would just be nice to have a fire you know. A little light in case someone needs to step out and go to the bathroom or something," said Sody, shifting uneasily in his seat. A long pause forced Sody to look over at Dakota. He was already asleep.

"Goodnight, Sodes," mumbled Chester. He curled up in a ball in the corner of the couch and quickly dozed off.

Sody sighed. "Goodnight, Chester."

Chester snored loudly back.

The fire quietly dwindled. The darkness from the corners of the cabin slowly crept in, tightening closer and closer and closer before swallowing the final source of light. The darkness, feeding and growing, feeding and growing.

Dakota's legs were outstretched, and his feet touched Sody, who sat at the intersection of the L-shaped mustard yellow couch. His feet smelled like they hadn't touched air in weeks. Sody, scrunching his nose in disgust, moved onto the floor next to Mocha. It was either that or die of asphyxiation by toe jam.

The rug in front of the fireplace may not have been anywhere near as comfortable as the couch but it would have to do for the night. Laying on his back he stared up at the Native chief, Busticogan, above the mantle. The picture was barely visible in the wake of the dying fire. The old chief's wrinkles appeared deeper. The bags under his eyes larger and darker. And the eyes were sunken, black and waning. A face full of wisdom. A face worn ragged from time and war.

Then Sody began thinking of the story Dakota told about the creature and a chill swept swiftly through him, standing the hairs up on his neck. He couldn't help but think that the face in the picture above the mantle was him, that he was the one being worn ragged from time and war.

He snatched the book off the arm of the couch and chucked it into the pit of coals in the fireplace. He wanted nothing more to do with the creature or any other story in that decrepit book.

It smoked slowly at first, a deep greenish-yellow smoke billowed up and out the chimney. And then a corner lit up with a small flame. It spread around the border of the cover and soon all that showed was the face of the bald man smoking his pipe. The face smiled. A devilish smirk with rotten, bared teeth. The sight haunted him, but Sody could not stop staring at it. Not until the flames engulfed the whole book.

Finally, he thought to himself, *I did what Dakota should have done in the first place.*

Outside the wind picked up and howled ghostlike through the pines. It came in an instant with a deep, earthy howl. It sounded alive. It had been quiet until then. Mocha stirred abruptly from her slumber. Sody shuddered while his other comrades remained motionless, sleeping. He envied them.

The pages in the book in the fireplace began flipping open rapidly.

Whap! Whap! Whap! Whap!

One after another, after another of charred, blackened pages, until it flipped open to the picture of the creature. That page hadn't yet been burned. No, that page was clear as day. Sody's eyes froze on the wretched face, its skin falling off and then . . . a rancid odor wafted thickly across the room. Ever so slowly the fire closed in on the creature and finally swallowed it whole. The smell faded, the book crumbled, and the remaining light from the fire flickered out.

Poof!

Sody, clenching his chest, let out all the air in his lungs. It whooshed out like an untied balloon. He was so frozen with fear he had forgotten to breathe. The room was pitch black. He couldn't see his hand in front of his face. He laid his head down on Mocha's side and tried to relax. Outside the howl of the wind faded to a whisper, and then stopped altogether. The abandoned cabin silenced once and for all. Its secret finally exposed and destroyed and hopefully, Sody prayed, would some-day be forgotten.

The following morning Dakota and Chester were awakened by a loud scraping noise coming from inside the cabin.

"Dude . . . what are you doing?" croaked Dakota, wiping the sleep from his eyes.

"Shoveling out the fireplace," Sody said. "I burned that book last night. Now I'm burying the ashes out back." He jammed the shovel into the ashes and dumped them into a metal pail.

"Don't you think that's a bit excessive?" asked Dakota.

"Not after last night. Not in the least bit. This book . . . or what's left of it, needs to be gone. Buried and forgotten."

"He's right," added Chester, "there was something about that book that just creeped me out. Thanks for doing that, Sodes. You did us all a favor, and anyone else who might have come across it."

Dakota sat up in his seat and stretched his arms behind his head. Mr. Chill. "I'm telling you guys, you're overreacting. That book was harmless. Just some playful horror stories is all."

Chester stared him right in the eyes and said, "Hey Dakota, just because you like flirting with danger, doesn't mean we do. What is it with you? I'm all for being daring and reckless and telling scary stories every now and again, but sometimes you take it too far, man. Don't you ever think about how other people feel? How your *friends* feel?"

And that was the end of the conversation. Chester didn't get defensive very often, but when he did, people knew not to mess with him. Dakota and Sody knew this all too well.

CHAPTER 11

Boys Will Be Boys

From the top of the ridge, the three boys gazed upon miles of lush green forest that surrounded Lake Napoleon. Chester sat cross-legged in the grass picking handfuls of the green strands, piling them up in a mound in front of him.

"What do you suppose *that* is?" he said pointing across the bay.

The three looked on in utter amazement. On the other end of the bay, clouds as black as soot swirled menacingly. Lightning forked and crisscrossed every which way and a faint low rumble riddled their bones.

Sody spoke while crossing his arms. "I think I have an idea about what it is."

"Fill us in," pleaded Dakota.

Sody stood up and tried to gather himself. He didn't like talking about his problems to anybody, especially his friends. He couldn't explain why, it was just the way he was. The way a lot of people are. "Well, you see . . . the day before I met up with you guys on the shoreline, I was walking down the road alone when I first saw it."

"Saw what?" retorted Chester and Dakota in unison.

"That!" Sody pointed at the storm. "I was standing on the Washkish when I saw a sign that pointed down Ringleader Road. I couldn't decide if I should go down it or not when I noticed that storm. The sky opened up like you wouldn't believe. Walls of rain and hail closed in on me from both directions. It was like the storm was alive. . . . That's when I dove into the tunnel. And then it shut behind me."

"What shut?" squeaked Chester.

"The tunnel. Everything went dark for a while, but eventually it cleared up and then I found you guys." Sody gazed at the ground looking completely zoned out. "Thankfully I found you guys."

Chester stood up from his spot in the grass. "That's really strange. Why do you think it's back? And why is it over there?"

As much as Sody hated talking about it, he felt like it actually helped confiding in somebody. *Strange*, he thought to himself. "I can't be certain, but I think I have to go back through it to get home. I think it's waiting for me."

Sody peered down the steep ridge to the lake. Most of the ridge below was bare rock. It sloped steeply down to the shoreline, nearly absent of any vegetation except for the grass at the top and a few hardy cedars that somehow rooted themselves into crevices in the rocks.

"Let it wait, Sodes," Dakota finally said, putting his arm around Sody. "Don't worry about it. Let's stop trekking for a bit. Maybe cool off in the lake for a while. Wuddaya say?"

"Great minds think alike," replied Sody.

A dip in the lake did sound pretty good. The sun was sweltering and sitting atop the ridge with no shade felt like being in a sauna.

"Guys look, a rope swing!" exclaimed Chester. He had wandered to the edge of the ridge and noticed it.

Sody walked up closer to Chester to take a look. "I don't see anything."

"It's right there!"

Sure enough, along the ridge where it gradually sloped back down to the forest was a long, knotted rope hanging from the branch of a Norway pine.

Dakota put his hands on the shoulders of Sody and Chester. "You guys thinking what I'm thinking?"

They both nodded in unison before all three blasted along the ridge towards the rope swing. Rocks and pebbles and small boulders tumbled down the side below their feet and splashed into the water. Their legs chugging like pistons in an engine, pumping at blinding speeds. Their arms did likewise, and it could be argued that nothing is quite as fast as adolescent boys in a foot race. Nothing.

"I won!" said Dakota.

"No way, that was totally a tie," replied Sody.

"Well technically it's nearly impossible to get an *exact* tie," stated Chester matter-of-factly. "One of us was likely the outright winner."

"Alright, Einstein, thanks for the math lesson," chirped Dakota.

"Actually, it's not math, it's—"

"Let's just call it a tie, okay guys? We're all really, really fast. Probably faster than anyone in the whole middle school." Sody bragged.

The woods went hush. Even the songbirds quit tweeting.

"You're lucky the eighth and ninth graders didn't hear that . . . they'd definitely challenge us to a race," warned Chester, eyes wide as cannon balls. He looked around to make sure no one heard the vilification that just came from his best friend's mouth.

"And we'd beat all of'em." Dakota grabbed the knot on the rope. "We'd beat all of'em any day of the week."

And then he leapt off. He sailed out beyond the rocky slope. The rope brought him inches from the water's surface and then swung him like a pendulum up and up into the thick July air. For just a moment he hung in one spot, peaceful and statue still. The way things do when you want to remember. And then he let go, silently. The whole world cave quiet as the rope sagged slowly back to shore and Dakota fell gracefully into the clear, blue void.

Splooosh.

Next it was Chester and finally, Sody's turn.

Sploosh.

Sploosh.

Into the clear, blue void.

The water felt cool in the midday heat. It refreshed the body and awakened the soul. Something about being in the water creates a primal feeling of freedom. Time slows. Responsibilities are swiftly forgotten. And the slow rush of aliveness creeps in like magic. Out in the water one cannot hear the busyness of land. No drone of an airplane. No buzz of a chainsaw. All one hears is the ancient ebbing and flowing of water created by the droplets of many rains, snowfall and underwater springs.

One becomes immersed in a piece of the past. Sody felt this and so he let himself sink slowly towards the bottom of Lake Napoleon. The water was colder down there. It caressed his skin, like ice to a burn. He gently closed his eyes and relaxed in the water's grip.

Up above on the surface, Chester and Dakota began to worry.

"He's been down there a long time," said Chester.

Dakota kicked his legs and arms and spun around while treading water. "Maybe he landed funny. We should probably go check on him." He sucked in a deep breath of air before plunging down to the depths. Chester followed closely behind.

Sody had been down there for almost a full minute. He trained all summer with Keegan, each trying to see who could hold their breath underwater for the longest time. *Keegan would be impressed now*, Sody thought.

Dakota could see his friend resting on the sandy bottom of the lake with arms and legs crossed like he was meditating. *What in the world is he doing?* He thought to himself. *He looks like a skinny Buddha.*

Chester wondered the same thing because he shot Dakota a confused look and shrugged his shoulders. The two swam the rest of the way down to save their friend. Sody's eyes flicked open instantly as both friends gripped tightly on either arm and dragged him back to the surface.

"Huhhhp!" Sody gulped up a mouthful of fresh air as soon as they pulled him to the top. "Forty-four seconds!"

"What!?"

"Forty-four seconds. That's how long I held my breath underwater for."

Chester rolled his eyes. "Really? That's what you were doing down there? Holding your breath?"

"Exactly. What'd you think I was doing?"

"We thought you were hurt," chimed Dakota. "Hence, the reason we pulled your sorry self to the surface."

"I think I coulda gotten sixty. Mmm . . . sixty-five maybe if not for your guys' *help*," said Sody holding up air quotations. "Either way, that's a record for me. I'm tired of treading water though, race you to shore."

And off they raced.

Soon, all three basked joyfully in the sun on shore. The day was still stifling hot and it did not take long to dry. Mocha, who had been waiting patiently on shore while they swam, also sunned herself. The rays glistened cleanly off her chocolate brown coat.

"Well fellas. Let's do this. Let's head back up to Ringleader Road and start trekking again. Gotta get back home at some point I spose," said Sody.

"Spose!" agreed Chester.

Dakota grumbled some and reluctantly dragged himself up from his peaceful spot on the rock. "Yeah, yeah . . . spose, spose, spose."

Sody looked off to the horizon in the west. "And plus, the sun is starting to set so we should find some sort of shelter for the night."

"How 'bout that abandoned cabin?" added Dakota smirking.

Sody and Chester locked eyes and simply shook their heads.

Back on the road Sody felt a bit more confident. He had his best friends and his lab by his side. It felt nice to not be alone. It was nice to have support.

The sun quietly sunk below the trees, leaving the sky a palate of red-golds and orange-yellows. Another stunning summer sunset. They marched in single file as the trail narrowed too much to allow for side-by-side walking. Mocha waddled out front as usual, followed by Chester, Sody and finally Dakota, taking up the rear. It was oddly quiet amongst them for the day had been long and they were well beyond ready to set up camp for the night.

It was nearly dark when Chester found them a promising spot. "What about here? We'd have the lake on one side of us and the trail on the other. It looks pretty decent don't ya think?"

"Not gonna lie, it does look pretty cozy up under those trees," agreed Sody with hands on his hips.

"I'll go grab some balsam boughs for us to lay on for the night, guys." added Dakota. He tossed Sody his zippo lighter. "Make yourself useful and get a fire going will ya?" He winked and dashed off into the night.

"Gotta love that guy," chuckled Sody.

Chester picked up a dry log and cradled it in one arm. "He is something else, isn't he?"

Chester gathered firewood while Sody collected some rocks to make a small fire ring. It didn't take long before Chester loaded the campsite with enough firewood to last a week. He also gathered several handfuls of birchbark which Sody methodically placed into the middle of the fire ring and started stacking small twigs around it.

"That looks cool. It's like a mini house," said Chester, peering over Sody's shoulder.

"It's a log cabin. My grandpa taught me how to make fires like this. Says it always works. Every time. Just have to make sure there is enough space between the sticks so that oxygen can flow through."

"I guess we'll see. By the way, it's been a while since Dakota went looking for boughs. Do you think he's alright?"

"Geez, I almost forgot about him," Sody admitted, looking beyond the campsite into the surrounding woods. "Maybe we should go look for him. I hope he didn't get lost or something."

The boys lit a small fire inside the ring of rocks before they left so they knew where to come back to in the dark. Sody beckoned his dog to stay put. Mocha happily slumped down next to the fire and rested her head on her front paws. She was worn out from the day's adventures. As Sody and Chester ventured off into the dark woods, Dakota peeked out from behind a tree on the other side of the fire. He had been back for a while watching his friends get the fire going, waiting for them to go looking for him.

He scrambled into the campsite, dropped off an armload of balsam boughs, then trailed giddily after his friends who were out looking for him.

"Dakota!" Chester bellowed.

"Dakota, where are you?" called Sody.

They could not find their friend anywhere. Chester's eyes strained, looking for any sign of movement. His heart started to pound faster, and a sinking feeling spread throughout his gut. The night quickly became nearly pitch black, with only the dim light from the moon to guide them.

"What the heck man? He should have answered by now," whispered Sody.

"This is bad. This is very bad, Sodes. What if something got him? Like. . ." Chester trailed off.

"Don't say i—"

"The creature."

"Oh, come on, Chester. I thought we weren't going to talk about that anymore," hushed Sody. "Now you're getting me all scared. Tell you what, let's go back to the campfire, maybe he'll be ba—"

A rustling came from the thickets behind them and they both shot around to face whatever it may be. However, it was far too dark to see what made the sound. Then a thud came from their left side. It sounded like something knocking on a tree. They slowly crept over to where the thud came from. Sody reached for his knife. His mind played visions of the creature, and then worse, of the spirit from his grandpa's story. The great ghastly monster. He dare not say its name. Could it be? Was it here to take him and his friends? It must have already gotten Dakota.

"Who's there?" Sody shouted as intimidating as he could muster. But he shook quietly with fear. "What do you want with us?"

"Sodes, maybe we should head back to the fire. Maybe Dakota is back there already."

"I don't know, something is off. He should have answered us by now. If he was within earshot, he would have answered. Maybe you are right. Maybe something *did* get him."

Sody and Chester exchanged frightened gazes. They crept closer to where they had heard the thud. Quietly, they peeked their heads around a tree and that is when they felt it.

Cold hands clutched each of them at the nape of their necks.

"AHHH!" Chester bolted, screaming bloody murder, crashing away blindly through the woods.

Sody could not move. He froze with the fear of the cold hand on his neck and the sudden realization that the spirit of the north wind had finally caught up to him. It's over. He imagined turning around and staring into the cold, empty eyes and smelling the rotting flesh. He remembered what his grandfather had said.

"Its eyes burned a hole into my soul."

Sody did not want to see its eyes, so he squeezed his own shut as tight as he could and prayed it would leave him alone.

Prayed something would save him. He felt its face creep next to his ear. Felt its icy breath on his cheek.

"Boo," said the voice into Sody's ear.

He wheeled around. It was Dakota! Sody tackled him hard to the ground.

"You jerk! You scared the crap out of us!"

Dakota rolled around on the ground laughing hysterically.

"I'm sorry, I'm sorry. I had to. It was too easy," he gasped between laughs.

After they both had gathered their composure, Dakota spoke. "We better go get Chester. He's probably in the next county by now."

Sody smiled at the thought of Chester high kneeing it out of there, but he was still rattled. He slugged Dakota on the shoulder before pulling him onto his feet.

"Let's go find that scaredy cat," chuckled Sody. He wasn't about to admit to Dakota that he was just as scared as Chester.

After finding Chester fifty yards away huddled under a fallen log, they trudged back to the fire laughing about the scare. They arrived to see the fire burned down to red hot coals and Mocha sleeping peacefully next to it. She rested a lot ever since the ant escapade. Sody gently laid a few more logs onto the fire while Dakota and Chester set to work arranging balsam boughs into bed mats. The logs took flame almost instantly and soon an orange glow flickered off the surrounding trees. The woods were quiet except for the crackle of fire.

Sody laid back on his bed of boughs and smiled. They had a fire and they had each other and that was enough. He fell asleep as soon as his head hit the ground. It had been a long day, but tomorrow would prove to be even longer.

CHAPTER 12

Alone

Sody awoke in the middle of the night to find both his friends gone. He got up and searched around the campsite for them, calling their names at the top of his lungs. He peered behind the looming trees on the outskirts of the campsite thinking perhaps they were hiding behind one. Still, he could not find them. In a panic, he whistled and whistled as loud as he possibly could. Nothing. He kept calling their names.

Then something started thrashing far off in the woods. It came closer and closer, and the thickets began rustling.

"You guys scared me. I thought you left!" huffed Sody with a sigh of relief.

Except neither Dakota or Chester came crashing through the woods, but rather his chocolate lab, all full of briars and burrs. Her tongue lolled out the side of her mouth. She trudged right past Sody and plopped down into the shallows of the lake, lapping at the water with her tongue. The light from the full moon shone off her coat and the ripples she made on the surface of the water.

"Where have *you* been?"

Sody called his dog. She paid no attention and continued lapping up water from the lake and walking slow circles in the cool water. He shrugged and turned to grab his canteen that sat on its side by the dying fire. That was when he saw the note on his bag. Scribbled on a hunk of birchbark with a shard of charcoal. In Dakota's handwriting, it read:

Dear Sodes,

We didn't want to leave like this but we have our own trials to attend to now. Yer ready now for whatever lies ahead. And remember, help comes to those who ask for it.

Friends forever,

Chester and Dakota

He really was alone now. With his friends gone, Sody again experienced a powerful feeling of anxiety coursing through his body. It terrified him being isolated again. Luckily, he still had Mocha to keep him company, but the absence of human companionship frightened him, making his stomach turn upside down. He hated the feeling. He hated how debilitating his anxiety could sometimes be and how it often came upon him unannounced, like a thief in the night. He hated how one moment he was fine and the next so nervous and agitated he didn't want to face the day. And tonight, of all nights, when he was finally ready to return home, it felt stronger than ever. Sody felt sick. A hot uneasiness coursed through his body like the flu and his stomach started to churn. He clambered into the woods so his dog wouldn't see him get sick and emptied the contents of his stomach. It didn't make him feel any better, which left him frustrated. His feelings transformed into despair and self-pity. Finally, he walked back to his bed of balsam boughs and collapsed in a heap. He never thought a person could feel so alone.

That's when he heard the manidoog.

"Ahh . . . Sody," they chided him, "right now, you are only thinking about yourself and your own problems. Your friends have their own lives. You must remember that. Look up at the sky and gaze upon the stars. Do you feel that? Can you feel your problems shrinking? The universe is vast, the world is as well. Your problems are small in the grand scheme of things. Don't you let your worries get the best of you."

Sody stood in the black of night, neck craned to the stars. It took him a short while, but as he breathed slowly in and out, his troubles slowly and silently melted away. And as his worries left him like river foam floating along after a set of rapids, a slow shiver ran across his skin. The shiver that comes when you realize it is okay. It is *all* okay, and, at least for a while, all the bad is forgotten.

He closed his eyes and sucked in a deep breath through his nostrils, tasting every bit of the cool summer night air flow into his lungs. He smelled it too. That wild summer scent that carries hints of the forest, the lake, a dying fire, and a dash of calm.

"Thank you," spoke Sody aloud into the night sky, "thank you."

And all started to feel well again.

He laid back down and swiftly drifted off into a deep, dreamless sleep. A regretless slumber.

The following morning, he woke up to Mocha licking his face.

"I'm glad you're still here, old girl. I don't know what I would do without you." Sody sat up to pet his twelve-year-old tail-wagger. Almost immediately she flipped onto her back expecting a belly rub, which she got.

"You're something else, you know that? A spoiled pooch, but I love you."

Mocha wiggled around on her back in the grass, jaws agape with her tail wagging frantically.

He couldn't help but laugh at the frantic excitement of his dog. A smile stretched from one ear to the other. The anxiety he experienced the night before when his friends disappeared had faded.

"That's good, Sody. That's good," the voice of the manidoog whispered into his ears. "You see clearer when your head isn't full of worry or fear. It's not always easy, as we surely know, but you must stay positive, stay curious. Ahh, yes . . . always stay curious, Sody."

"Stay curious," muttered Sody, repeating what the manidoog had said. He always considered himself a very curious person. He wanted to know everything about anything and anything about everything. A blessing and a curse. Sometimes it got him into trouble. Sometimes, however, it showed him new places and ideas. New perspectives.

He walked down to the shoreline and dipped his canteen into the water. The lake was still, and he could see his reflection looking back at him in the water. He stared at it for some time. He looked older now. Wiser perhaps. A smile lifted from the corner of his mouth and he marched back up to the campsite and doused the fire with the water from his canteen. The coals hissed and the cold smoke from the ashes lifted and quickly disappeared.

"Come on, Mocha, let's go home."

Woo-woof! *Okay, Sody!*

They left the campsite and marched down Ringleader Road. The day was getting hot, but a stiff breeze knocked back the brunt of it. Pine needles littered the forest floor and filled the air with a wonderful forest aroma. Mocha and Sody walked through a gorgeous grove of red pines that lined the shore. The trail snaked through the pines back towards the camper. He could tell they were getting close. They might make it home today. The thought fueled Sody, and he broke into a jog, but that wasn't enough. Soon he sprinted, and Mocha kept up right by his side. Butterflies danced around in his stomach. He had purpose. And that is all a person needs.

Just up the trail an ancient white pine loomed over the rest of the trees. A lone white pine in a sea of Norways. Although Sody had climbed his fair share of trees during his childhood, none of them compared to this one. It must have stood over one hundred feet high and was likely three hundred years old or better. Among the many giant white pines that lined Lake Napoleon, it was clearly the largest. As he approached the tree it became impossibly more impressive. Its lower branches were the size of most trees and lucky enough for Sody, they were just within reach.

Soon enough the tree was right in front of him. He grabbed for the lowest branch and when he did, noticed a poem etched into the trunk of the tree.

CLIMB ME AND YOU SHALL SEE

I'M A TREE LIKE THE BEANSTALK,

A GIANT'S KNEE

LEAVE YOUR WORRIES AT MY BASE

SO YOU CAN CLIMB WITHOUT A BRACE

How curious, he wondered. So as not to offend the tree, Sody indeed left his worries at the base, where they soaked into the ground and into the very roots of the tree which transformed into an overwhelming rush of fresh oxygen that Sody sucked in with one giant deep breath. Ahhh. Out with the old, in with the new. Nature is cleansing like that.

He hoisted himself up onto the lowest branch. "You gotta stay here now, Mocha. I'll be right back, I promise."

While her master climbed from branch to branch, Mocha sat and watched patiently. She was as loyal as the day is long, that is, until a squirrel or chipmunk crossed her path. Then all bets were off. Her ears perked up as she heard chattering far off in the thick woods.

The higher Sody climbed, the better the view became. Once over the canopy of the smaller trees, he was able to see the rest of the lake. He noticed all the different bays and coves. The streams that flowed gracefully in and out and the gravel pit where he and his friends battled the ants, and yes, even the abandoned cabin. A chill flushed through Sody's body when he saw the cabin and recalled the creature. He quickly looked away to see what lie ahead.

The storm still lived and rumbled. It was close now. Sody swallowed. He had to brave it one more time. There, however, just beyond the storm, off in the distance across the bay, stood the camper. His heart fluttered. How he longed to be home. He could see the smoke rising from the fire pit near the camper. *I wish they could see me. I wish they could see how far I've come.* He *had* come far indeed. In fact, he figured he was close to completing his journey around the lake.

Then a thought struck him. *How come, after all this time, there had never once been a boat out on the lake?* His dad never came out looking for him, nor had any other boat. This troubled him. He felt abandoned. *Had they really cared so little as to not come looking for me, even once?*

The voice of the manidoog floated in like a soft breeze. "You must remember Sody. You are in your own world right now. And they are in theirs. Of course, they came and looked for you. Many times, and by many different means, but they could never find you because you did not want to be found."

Sody looked around, trying to get a glimpse of the manidoog, to see where the voice came from. He knew deep down the manidoog were not something or somebody that could be seen.

"You mean if I wanted to be found, they could find me? It's that simple?" he asked.

"Well . . . yes, in a way, but it is not so simple at the same time. As you have seen on your journey, to get back home you have encountered many obstacles, none of which were easy."

"I know, but I got through all of them." Sody spoke to the wind.

"With help you did. Now you must finish this alone. You're nearly there."

He imagined leaping from the branch and taking flight like an eagle—the great migizi. Flying over treetops, soaring on the wind, and finally reaching home. Getting home was all that mattered now. It was time. He saw what he needed to see. Felt what he needed to feel. Learned what he had come to learn. Getting home was all that mattered now.

He soaked in the last few moments of the incredible view before clambering back down the tree. As he reached the bottom, he realized Mocha had disappeared. Surprise, surprise!

"Mocha! Come here girl!"

Silence.

He waited a few more minutes before calling her again. Still nothing. Sody's heart beat a little faster. He tried whistling. Nothing. Not a stir. *Well, I'll just keep walking. Maybe she'll turn up eventually.*

Determined and motivated beyond measure, he got back on the road. It felt good to have a goal to chase. It kept him honest with himself. It kept him fighting. And the goal now was to finish his journey, to get through the storm. Then after that he would make some more goals. And more after that. Everyone should always have a goal, he believed. All the time. Life should be as simple as that. Now the thought of living without purpose irked him. There had to be something to always look forward to or improve upon.

Once back on Ringleader Road he called for his dog once more. Mocha was nowhere to be seen. A small pit gathered in the bottom of his stomach. She'd done this a few times before—ran off chasing heaven knows what, but she always came back. He had to believe that. He picked up his pace to a jog. It felt right. He headed straight for the storm. The new Sody was ready.

This section of the trail was different from the rest. Less traveled. The grass stood knee high, and the trail was far narrower and more rugged. It appeared nobody had traveled through it in quite some time. *Maybe that's because they never made it this far,* Sody thought. The realization gave him more motivation to keep on. The storm boomed deeply just ahead. A flash of green lightning streaked across the blackened clouds.

"Nearly there, Sody. You are ready. You can do it. Don't forget that," whispered the manidoog.

"I'm ready," he said aloud. Somehow, saying it out loud made it feel more real. He believed in himself.

At a bend in the trail, he lay witness to a wall of rain from the approaching storm. Just like the day he first saw it. *I'm not going to run from you now. I'm going to make you disappear.* Sody unstrapped the backpack from his shoulders and held it up over his head.

"One . . . two . . . three!" he shouted, sprinting straight into the wall of rain.

The pouring rain soaked him, and he recalled the day before he moved out of his former house in Togo earlier in the summer when a different storm had done the same. Sody smiled. The thunder boomed overhead, and lightning flashed so brightly it illuminated millions of droplets of rain in the darkness. *How beautiful.* Somehow his feet kept him on the path, although his eyes could not see it.

The sound of the rain drowned out all other noises.

CHAPTER 13

Back on the Homefront

Keegan sat at the top of the fort he had helped build just weeks before. He peered through dusty binoculars searching for any sign of his brother—scanning the shorelines and woods, but no luck. Just before he gave up, however, he noticed something across the bay of the lake. It floated on top of the water, the waves rocking it gently back and forth against the shoreline. Keegan's heart sank. He put the binoculars down abruptly. Whatever was floating in the water, he wasn't sure he wanted to know.

"I thought you might be up here."

Keegan jumped so hard he almost fell out of the fort. Drew had climbed up to keep him company and Keegan hadn't taken notice.

"What's wrong? Looks like you've seen a ghost," said Drew.

Keegan didn't answer.

"*Did* you see a ghost?"

He shook his head and handed the binoculars over to Drew, pointing out at the floater across the bay. Drew's stomach tightened up instantly. Could it be? Was it their brother washed up along the shoreline? He slowly lifted the binoculars to his eyes. It took him a little while to find it, but sure enough, there it was. The floater. Drew wiped off the dust from the lenses to see clearer.

Finally, his stomach slackened. It wasn't Sody. Rather, a large birch log knocking against the shoreline. He exhaled and handed the binoculars back to Keegan.

"It's okay Keegan, it's just a log. Here, take a look for yourself. I promise, it's just a log."

Keegan, unconvinced, nudged his face up against the eyepieces. He put the binoculars down and stared out over the lake.

"Where do you think he is? Do you think he's okay?"

It took Drew a moment to find the right words to say to his youngest brother.

"If I know Sody at all, he's okay. And if he's not okay, if he's lost, he will find his way eventually. Right now, we've done all we can. And honestly Keegan, I think he's just lost, and I know it might sound weird, but I think he wanted to be."

Keegan stared Drew in the eyes. "I hope you're right. I'm scared for him."

Drew did his best to force a convincing smile. *I hope I'm right too*, he thought.

Just then, a vehicle pulled up to the camper and a car door slammed shut. It was impossible to see who it was through the trees so Drew shimmied down the ladder and headed back towards the camper. Keegan remained perched on the fort and prayed silently to the skies.

"Drew, hey. How ya doin' kid?" It was their Grandpa George.

"Hi Grandpa. I'm doing alright." He looked down at his feet. "As good as I can I guess."

His grandpa patted him fatherly on the shoulder. "Your parents around? Haven't heard from them in a while. People have been asking questions. Heck, your grandma and I have our own questions too." He looked around the lot. No campfire going. No towels hanging on the line. It appeared everyone was missing, not just Sody.

"Ye-yeah. They're around. I think my mom is sleeping, and my dad is out driving around with Jaime looking for Sody. He's always out driving around."

"Alright, well I won't bother them." His voice sounded strained. "Just tell them I stopped in and want to talk to them as soon as possible." He started back towards his rusted out, white Chevy pick-up.

As he pulled on the handle to get into his truck, the camper door clanged open, and Shelly stepped gingerly out. Her hair was in disarray, and she wore no makeup. She looked haggard, tired and worried.

"Shelly . . . hey, I uh, I just stopped in quick to see how you all were doing. I-I didn't mean to wake you," said George.

"You're fine George, come on in. I'll put some coffee on."

They went inside. Shelly handed him a coffee mug. He was visibly nervous. His hand trembled as he brought the mug to his lips, so he used his other to steady it. He watched as Shelly attempted to pour herself a cup. She spilled some on the floor and George heard her curse under her breath.

"Listen, Shelly, if you want to go back to b—" George started.

"I'm fine," she interjected a little more coldly than she intended. "Sorry. It's just, Sody being gone has been hard on all of us. I don't even know where to start."

"He's out there somewhere, Shelly. I can feel it."

Shelly quietly nodded her head and tears welled up in the corners of her eyes. She stood over the coffee pot. George got up from his seat and patted her on the back. "Things have a way of working out. Even when they really don't seem like they will. How's Dario doing? Drew said he was out with Jaime."

"He goes out every day with her. There's no sign of Sody anywhere and nobody on the lake has seen hide nor hair of him. I think maybe he keeps looking to keep his mind off of . . . well, you know."

"You can't think like that, Shelly. You just can't."

"I know, I know. It's just sometimes you can't help it, you know?" She brought her coffee mug to her lips, then reconsidered. "You try and try to figure out where he might be and why he left and at the end of the day all you have is unanswered questions. This is all just so awful, George."

Just then, Drew peeked his head inside the camper. "Dad and Jamie are back. They just pulled in."

"Hey Pops. It's been a while," said Dario as George carefully stepped out of the camper.

"You're telling me. How ya been? Your mom and I have been thinking about you guys. She wanted to come with, but I wouldn't let her. Last week she took a little spill off the deck. Tweaked her knee, but enough about—"

"Is she alright? I feel terrible we haven't been by in some time," said Dario sadly.

"It's fine, really, she's fine. Any word? Any news at all about Sody?"

Dario let out a long exhaustive sigh. "Nothing. Unfortunately. But we're trying. Lord knows we're trying." He did his best to look optimistic, but it was obvious he needed some rest. "What have people around town been saying?"

"Well. . ." George started.

"Actually, you know what, I don't even want to know. I don't care to know. You and Mom must have questions though. I'm sorry we haven't been keeping touch."

"Don't be sorry. We get it. No one imagined anything like this ever happening. Especially to one of *your* kids." George looked his son in the eyes. "You and Shelly are great parents. Don't ever think you're not. You raised good kids. Now we gotta find your boy."

Out across the bay a storm emerged. Its blue-black clouds promised peril. The Fairbanks saw it and felt the staleness in the air. That charged air that only comes when a fierce squall is on the horizon. Dario peered over to the picnic table where Jaime sat by herself. She took a break from writing in her journal and gazed out over the lake. Strands of her hair rose up weightlessly and hovered in mid-air around her head. Charged air.

The surface of Lake Napoleon looked like polished glass. The calm before the storm. The Fairbanks family had no clue their son was out there, just across the bay, in the middle of the storm. They were completely unaware he was fighting it alone. They couldn't know. Sody was fighting with his whole heart to get home to them. And no one knew because he could never tell them.

"I better be off. Don't want to get caught in that." George nodded towards the storm.

"We'll see ya Dad," replied Dario with arms crossed, "thanks for stopping by."

George rumbled off down the drive and as he did the wind picked up considerably. Dario paced down to the lake and grabbed two tubes and a swim noodle that were strewn about on the grass. It struck him that there wasn't another tube or another noodle lying there. Sody's tube had been stashed back in the shed. He looked out at the lake with glassy eyes. He hoped his son was out there somewhere, hoped he would come back. He couldn't help but feel guilty. And the guilt crushed him.

What a storm, he thought, *what a storm.*

CHAPTER 14

The Light at the End of the Tunnel

The storm was menacing. It scowled far worse this time around, and something about it was different. This time he felt ready for it. Sody knew how to weather it. Or so he thought.

It wasn't just the rain that soaked him to the core. Or the thunder that rattled his bones. The wind howled straight down the road, screaming like a runaway freight train, knocking him backwards. He dropped to his hands and knees and crawled forward. Whatever it took. He used the rocks and roots to pull himself along. Inch by inch. Foot by foot. Rain water pooled up all around him. So much rain. He craned his head up at the sky and let out a raucous, primal laugh.

"HAAHAAA! WHOOOO! Bring it on! Give me whatever you got!" he yelled.

A few more feet further and the wind slowed considerably. The rain lightened up and the rumbling of thunder seemed to fade into the distance.

Sody stood up and looked behind him to see the wall of rain continue down the shoreline of the lake with little flashes of lightning and low rumbles of thunder.

I knew I could do it.

"Nearly there, Sody. One more test," said the manidoog.

"What do you mean? The storm. . ." he trailed off, looking all around him. "I thought that was the final test."

The wind was sucked out of his sails.

"We know. We know far too well how badly you want to get home. Keep your head up, eyes forward. You made it this far. Now go prove your worth," said the manidoog.

As much as he wanted to quit. As much as he just wanted to be home eating a home cooked meal, holding his family, he knew he was so close, and he didn't make it this far to just roll over and quit.

He tousled his matted hair the rain had soaked, re-tied his shoes, and kept on. His eyebrows furrowed deeply. Nothing could stop Sody Fairbanks now. Maybe the old Sody, but not the new one. He was different now.

That's when he felt the earth begin to quake, just slightly. He thought maybe it was just the remnants of the storm passing, but he was wrong. This proved to be something far more sinister. It came from underneath him. He stopped in his tracks afraid to lose his balance. It became more and more apparent. More and more concerning. He looked around for answers but found none.

Slowly, thick trees emerged out of the soil around him. Balsam firs and spruces and jack pines all intertwined with branches twisting together to box him in. He stood there speechless, frozen in his shoes. Only his neck and head moved as he gazed upon the impossible spectacle surrounding him. Before he could even think of what was going on, the jagged trees reached nearly ten feet in height and the tops snarled inward to form a sealed dome above him. Darkness. Everything went black. And cold. The warmth of the sun could not penetrate the cage of trees. Sody found himself alone dripping in cold sweat. Trapped by an unknown force.

He had wondered what the manidoog had meant when they said he had one more test to pass.

Now he knew.

The spirit of the north wind had come.

Sody banged on the wall of trees before him, but they were far too dense to budge.

"Hello?" he shouted into the dark.

The word got absorbed by the trees and only came out a whisper. He heard something rustle in the leaves behind him. He whipped around to face it but still saw nothing.

"Who's there?" Sody asked.

Again, the words were absorbed by the trees.

Sody raced around the perimeter of the forest cell searching for a way out. Nothing. No way out, no way in. He got on his hands and knees and tried crawling beneath the branches, but they stretched all the way to the ground. Next, he tried climbing to the top only to find the ceiling was just as solid as the walls.

He sat down against the wall of trees, panting. There had to be some way. He had to think, had to use what he learned on his journey. Something rustled once more in front of him. Still, he could not make out what it was or what it could be. Naturally, his mind presumed the worst possible scenarios. Maybe another bear. Maybe it was the creature from the book. Deep down, though, he knew what it was.

Sody knew it was the spirit of the north wind. The mind eater. He shuddered at the thought.

It rustled again. Closer this time.

His heart rate doubled. His breathing quickened.

"Please don't be the spirit, please don't be the spirit," he whispered.

He clasped his eyes shut, then opened them, thinking maybe it was all a dream. He would wake up at any moment. That's what it was. Just another nightmare like he had earlier in the summer after his grandpa first told him the story. Except he did not wake up.

It was not a dream. He squinted his eyes and could just make out what appeared to be a hand reaching out to him. *Is someone trying to help me*? He was about to reach his own hand out but before he did, he saw the eyes. The icy blue eyes from his grandpa's story. And then he smelled the putrid breath. It was here.

"Hello, my boy." Its voice was smoky, but impossibly calming.

It sounded almost inviting. *Curious*, thought Sody.

"H . . . hello," he answered feebly.

"I've been waiting for you. I thought you would never come. But!" The beast paused. "You have let me in nonetheless and for that I should thank you."

Sody was confused. He didn't recall the spirit talking in his grandpa's story.

"Le . . . let you in? I didn't let you in. What are you talking about? Don't come any closer."

"That is where you are wrong, my boy. You let me in, you just don't know it. But it doesn't matter now because here I am. And here you are. There is nowhere to go now. So just relax. Stay here with me awhile."

Sody felt uneasy. *Can I trust it?* The spirit in his grandpa's story seemed scarier than this one. Except for those eyes. Its eyes showed death. Sody's stomach twisted itself in a knot.

"I don't trust you. Stay away."

Only it came closer. Sody also noticed a faint blue glow coming from where he assumed its chest must be.

"Shh shh shhh. Hush. It's okay," the smoky voice whispered. "I won't hurt you. Here, let me help you up."

Sody's eyes adjusted to the blackness of his surroundings. An oversized, shadowed hand reached out for him. Long, spindly grey fingers protruded from a skeletal palm. He ducked under the spirit's reach and sprinted headlong into the wall on the other side of the entrapment.

Think, Sody, think.

"Silly boy. Not much room to run in here . . . or to hide. Soon you will find that this little dark room is allll you need. I can make all your problems go away. You won't have to worry anymore," persuaded the spirit of the north wind.

The beast strode effortlessly toward Sody and reached him in an instant. The dark room was small. Sody rushed to the other side and panic sunk in. Nowhere to go.

It chased after him again. Suddenly, its eyes glowed brighter. They dimly illuminated a face that was rotting away. Its nose was missing and there a crooked smile showed behind the holes in its cheeks.

"Relax, boy. There is nothing to be scared of here. Nothing can hurt you here." Its voice remained calm, despite Sody's efforts to escape.

Sody half believed it. Part of him wanted to collapse in a heap on the forest floor. He was exhausted. Completely drained of spirit. Sleep sounded wonderful. *Maybe I'll just sleep. I'll*

sleep, and it'll leave me alone and be gone when I wake up.
But he knew better than that. He knew if he didn't do something fast, he might never escape, and the thought scared him beyond measure.

Sody flailed and scratched and clawed at the wall of trees before he finally had to stop to take a breath. The spirit, as if entertained, watched him quietly. Sody scratched and clawed some more.

"Nooo! Let me out of here!" he yelled.

It snickered at him.

He wore his fingernails down until they bled. He was so close to home. The journey had taken him so far. And for what? To be stopped now?

"Sody, your knife." He stopped clawing at the wall realizing this advice didn't come from the manidoog this time. It came out of his own mouth, but it sounded the same. How curious.

Yes! That's it, he thought. *How could I be so stupid?* He fumbled hastily through his backpack. Tossing out his canteen in his desperate flailing. The knife had killed a bear, could it kill the spirit of the north wind as well?

"Got it." He held the small jackknife up in the air like it was the Excalibur sword.

"Got what? What is that in your hand?" The spirit, no longer entertained, sounded scared. Worriedly, it crept closer. It didn't like that its prey sensed hope.

Sody started inching toward the evil spirit. His confidence was back, and the spirit cowered backwards in disbelief. "What's wrong?" Sody asked. "How does it feel to be the one who is scared?"

He kept his eyes on the faint blue glow coming from the spirit's chest. He remembered what his grandpa had told him about killing spirits of the north wind. *You must shatter the heart, not just pierce it. Break it into as many pieces as you can.*

"You are nothing, boy. You really think you can kill a—"

Before the spirit could finish, Sody lunged. He cocked his arm back like he was swinging a hatchet and swung it down hard on the blue glow. The sound of a thousand vases shattering all at once echoed around the tight confines of the chamber. Shards of icy heart splintered into hundreds of tiny crystals, falling to the ground like wishless shooting stars.

As the pieces hit the floor, the earth began to rumble, and the forested walls surrounding him slowly crumbled to dust. Finally, he could see again. There was light! He immediately sprinted down the trail as fast as he could until he could run no more. An enormous weight lifted off his shoulders. He could breathe again. He doubled over, panting, and looked back to see if the spirit was somehow still alive and following him. To his amazement he witnessed what was left of the beast and the dome he had been trapped in evaporate into a black smoke and drift off dissipating into the bright blue sky. Drifting off like the spent tendrils of a dark dandelion wish.

He smiled. It was over. Then he looked up and saw that his feet had carried him to the edge of the tunnel. The tunnel that would bring him back to the camper and his family. Back to good. It was bittersweet, but mostly sweet. He could see far, far down to the end of the tunnel where, if he looked just hard enough, he could see a light.

He walked down the path and couldn't help but wonder how it would feel to be back home. Back at the camper. Back with his family. *Are they going to be mad at me?* Furious probably.

Sody kicked a rock off the path.

The farther he walked, the closer the trees got, tighter and tighter, choking out the light of the sun. This looked all too familiar to Sody. He remembered the exact opposite thing happening when he first began his journey down Ringleader Road.

It really wasn't so long ago. When the tunnel first opened up and the trees slowly gave way to the rays of the sun, and he found himself in this wonderfully exhilarating new world. He learned a lot during his journey. And now he was reaching the end. Sody recalled the riddle from the entrance to Ringleader Road.

WHAT YOU SEEK IS HERE, HIDDEN AND HARD.

FOR THOSE WHO FOLLOW, MOST WILL FAIL.

BUT THERE IS A REWARD, IF YOU DO GO FORWARD.

The riddle couldn't be more right. What he sought *was* hidden and hard, but he found it. Down Ringleader Road. Many times, he thought he would fail, but there was always help when he needed it most. And he always had himself when he needed himself most. That was perhaps the most important thing.

And finally, the reward. He smiled. It was funny how his view of the world changed since he first came upon the riddle. He thought the reward might prove to be endless riches or fame, like the pot of gold at the end of a rainbow. But the reward proved to be far more meaningful than any speck of gold or ounce of fame. He found *himself* down that road. He found what it meant to live–that happiness and fulfillment dwells within each of us, not from anything on the outside. And he also realized that sadness comes from the same place, inside us . . . That sadness comes from the same place.

He looked around and shrugged his shoulders. He dragged his hands through the balsam branches, inhaling their piney scent. It was time to go. With or without Mocha. He couldn't wait forever.

CHAPTER 15

Home

Sody picked up his pace. He rumbled through the tunnel like a raging bull moose. He was nearly home. He could smell it, could almost see it. His heart raced. Thump thump thump thump. Over a log, under a branch. Thump thump thump thump. His throat burned a fiery pain from having worked his body to its breaking point. Thump thump thump thump. The tunnel was starting to close ahead. *Oh no, I can't get stuck in here.* He refused to be trapped there forever. Branches and brambles grabbed at his clothes, untied his shoelaces, but he moved as quick as lightning, as powerful as thunder. The light was shrinking. Darkness everywhere.

"Jump, Sody," he whispered to himself.

He leapt with all his might.

Thhhip.

The tunnel shut, just like it had when he first entered the tunnel. Darkness. Silence.

Sody opened his eyes and found himself surrounded by a grove of tall cedar trees. The same grove he had entered to get out of the storm. Here the forest floor was thick with beaked hazel shrubs and alder. No wonder nobody had found him. He had crossed the barrier once more, back into the real world. He began working his way out of the ancient cedar swamp towards the road.

As he got back to the road, he could hear a faint familiar voice far off in the distance. "Kids, it's time to eat." It sounded like something from a dream or a distant memory. The muffled voice was his mother's. He sprinted as fast as he could, following the words to the driveway that led to the camper. They sounded so sweet, carried quietly to his ears upon an invisible breeze. When he got there, panting for air, he looked down at his hands, turning them over, then at his feet, he turned them out and back in. His shoes were filthy and soaking wet. *Did I actually make it out? It's impossible.* Surely, he'd felt he may be doomed to stay there forever. In the dark room . . . with the spirit of the north wind. Looking behind him he noticed nothing out of the ordinary. Just the woods on the other side of the road.

Looking forward, still gasping for air, he lifted his gaze. There she was. His Mom. Down at the end of the long drive she stood over the picnic table sorting blueberries. He tried to yell to her, but nothing came out. His stomach was in his throat. Tears welled in his tired eyes. His mouth dry like flour. She looked so lifeless.

"Mom," he whispered.

Suddenly, she looked up as if she heard him. Maybe the breeze carried his whisper to her or maybe she felt his presence, standing alone at the end of the drive. She ran toward him and he to her. Trembling at the sight of her lost son she stumbled to him, her sandy brown hair blowing softly in the breeze, tears streaming down her freckled face.

"Sody," she mouthed, but no words came out.

He peered up at his mom's face and saw what heartbreak does to a person. Her eyes were sunken. Her face thin and her hair beginning to gray, just slightly. Then her lips turned up in an incredibly wide smile. And her sharp blue eyes twinkled, not once, but twice in the high-noon sun.

"I'm sorry Mom," said Sody.

"Shhh . . . you're back now, hun . . . you're back now." She held him close, like she did when he was a baby. She spoke the words as if she couldn't believe them. "You have some explaining to do, but that can wait. For now, I'm just so glad you're home. We had search parties for you, you know. We looked everywhere. I thought maybe someone kid . . . ne . . . never mind. God, we all felt so sick, Sody."

She noticed the cuts and abrasions on him.

"And what happened to your side? Where did you get all these cuts?"

"Mom, I—"

"Don't. It's okay. Let's go find your dad and get you bandaged up. He has been a ghost since you've been gone. He felt responsible for . . . well, for you disappearing. All he kept saying was that it was his fault because you two were fighting the last time we saw you."

Sody's stomach dropped. Guilt flooded through him. He never thought about how badly his family would have been affected by his absence, especially since he and his dad had been on bad terms the day he found himself down Ringleader Road.

Dario stood in the kitchen in the camper when Sody and Shelly walked in. He loomed over the kitchen sink, staring down at the empty metal basin, his hands resting on it like he was trying to catch his breath.

"Dad!" Sody ran to his father, hugging him. Dario turned and took his son's face into his gentle hands.

It wasn't real. His son couldn't really be there. He was gone. Lost to the world. But it *was* real. Dario tried to speak but words failed him. He just stood there hugging his son. Suddenly the screen door on the camper blasted open and Drew, Jamie, and Keegan all clambered in.

"Sodes!" yelled Jamie.

All three siblings group hugged their brother. All the commotion and emotion overwhelmed Sody so much he burst into tears, crying into his dad's shirt.

"What's wrong Sodes? Why are you sad?" asked Keegan.

"I'm not sad, I'm very happy. Very, very happy."

"Why are you crying then?" Keegan was too young to understand that someone could cry and be happy at the same time.

"Sometimes people cry when they are happy. It's sort of tough to explain, but trust me, I'm glad to be back and see you guys."

"In that case, let's all go swimming!" squeaked Jamie.

"In a while," Sody explained. "I just need to see you all again, all together again. I am so glad to be home."

After a while, however, as tired as he felt, Sody found his swim trunks and went with his siblings down to the lake. He stood on the shoreline for a moment, soaking in the reality of being home. Oh, how good it felt! He smiled, then sprinted at full speed along the dock and jumped as far as he could into the cool blue water.

Sploosh.

Dario sat on the stiff, pink couch inside the camper. The air conditioner buzzed away above him. Holding his face in his hands, tears streaming. Shelly stood beside him rubbing his back, not saying a word.

He sniffled and shook his head. "It was all my fault . . . I . . . I shouldn't have been so hard on him. Oh, Shelly, it's all my fault."

"Shhh . . . it's not your fault. He's back now and that's what matters. It's okay," she said quietly, "our boy is back. You know better than anyone that it was only a matter of time before he had to spread his wings. He's going to move the earth that one. I think deep down you know that, and it scares you."

"This is why I married you. You know me all too well. I guess I . . . I don't know. I'm just so happy he's back. I was so lost. We were all so lost," said Dario.

He picked himself up and hugged his wife tightly. Then he let out a deep breath, walked over to the refrigerator and grabbed some lemonade. It was summer, after all. Summer on the lake in northern Minnesota. It doesn't get any better than that.

"Well, it's time to celebrate. Cheers! To our kids."

"To our kids," she answered with a smile.

CHAPTER 16

Miles to Go

A loon called from across the lake, singing to the setting sun. The lake was mostly still except for the ripples made by Sody's feet dangling off the end of the dock. He sat quietly looking out at the water, soaking in the enchantment of nature, the magic of summer.

His first day back, his family had hammered him with questions all afternoon before he managed to slip out to the dock. He was excited to see them and grateful to be back, but it was too much stimulation all at once. As the lake reflected the sky, Sody reflected upon his life.

After getting home from his journey into another realm, he realized he needed time alone to process all that had happened. It was one of the ways to discover who we truly are, the soul inside of us. We have to take long walks in the woods and sit on swings, watching the sunset while the sky changes colors. We have to climb trees and fall and sometimes get hurt. Jump in mud puddles while it rains and jump off docks as far as you can. That's how we find out what we are capable of.

Reflection, he thought, *we all need time to reflect.* Just like the lake sometimes reflects the sky and the trees that line the shoreline. And maybe we need to take time to think about the past and the future. Time to think about what really matters to us, and what doesn't matter at all. He recalled the many lessons his dad and grandpa taught him. Sody was sure he couldn't have finished his journey if not for their advice, if not for their wisdom. Sometimes, it's not always what we think about most, but what we think about the least, that will grant us happiness. If we spend our whole life focusing on our mistakes and faults and failures, we will not be able to get past them. Know them, learn from them, and move on. There is no glamor in pitying ourselves or looking for people to feel bad for us.

Sody felt the dock shift some and heard the dock boards behind him clop, clop, clop. He turned to see his younger brother, Keegan, coming towards him with a freezy-pop in each hand. Mocha trotted by his side.

"Mocha! Come here girl. I missed you." She flopped onto her back and Sody rubbed her belly, then wrestled her. "I can't believe you are back!"

He was certain the woods had gotten her. That she had gotten stuck in that other world when the tunnel shut. But here she was, as hyper and happy as ever. He almost questioned how she got back, but he was done questioning things for now. After what he'd seen, anything seemed possible.

"What color?" Keegan asked, holding out the freezies.

"I'll take the blue one."

Keegan handed him the blue freezy and started in on the pink one himself, his favorite.

"Mom said it's almost time for dinner," said Keegan while taking a seat next to his brother.

"What's she cookin'?" Sody put his feet back in the water.
"Everything. Like the whole kitchen is full. . . . Hey, Sodes. . ."
"Yeah?"

"I'm glad you're home. Really glad. We all missed you." Keegan
set his dirty feet in the water. He struggled to hold back tears.
"Mom and Dad were going crazy. Drew and Jamie had to keep
them together. I guess we thought you might never come back
and that scared us. . . . Why'd you go? Why did you just leave?"

"I'm really sorry Keegs. I felt like I had to, like something
was telling me to, you know?" Keegan watched Sody squint out
across the lake. "It might not make sense to you now, but I'm
sure someday it will. I know I would have regretted it if I never
went. But I'm sure glad I'm back, I missed you guys too. More
than you could imagine."

"Did you see lots of cool stuff?"

Sody tossed a rock he had been holding into the lake. "Boy,
did I. I saw lots of stuff I wouldn't have ever seen back here. And
I'll just leave it at that." Sody reached his arm across his younger
brother's shoulders and they sat in silence for a moment looking out at the lake. Sody felt the hairs prick up on the back
of Keegan's neck and his little brother looked up at him and
just smiled.

"Race you to the camper!" Keegan chirped and blasted off
up the hill. Sody followed suit, like a cheetah chasing a gazelle.
Mocha joined the race too. Their bare feet blurred over the fresh
cut July grass, running over the soft green blades of nature's carpet, going so fast the air felt cool on their faces and gushed over
their ears like a roaring gust of wind. It was over in seconds. The
rush of adrenaline subsided, and heartbeats mellowed.

"I think that's the first time I've ever beaten you!" exclaimed Keegan.

Sody tousled his brother's hair. "And it won't be the last. Let's go eat."

Inside, their mom had cooked up a beautiful feast. There was fry bread and wild rice and homemade meatballs and green beans and fresh corn and garlic bread and lettuce from the garden. She was so excited everyone was together so she cooked up just about everything from the fridge and her garden. Everything except the kitchen sink. Even a fresh baked apple crisp sat cooling on the counter. Sody's mouth watered. He hadn't eaten a home cooked meal in what seemed like an eternity. His stomach growled so loud everyone heard it.

"Your dad needs to say a prayer first before we dig in," she said. "Dario, say a prayer for us, our family, and for Sody's safe return."

And Dario said a prayer in Ojibwe. "Chii miigwech minobimaadiziwin." *(We are very thankful for this good life.)*

"Now eat up!" Shelly exclaimed.

Sody grabbed the largest plate he could find and heaped food so high he had to use two hands to balance it. Dario observed his son with a look of both utter amazement and concern.

"I hope your eyes aren't bigger than your stomach," he said.

Sody sat down on the recliner in the living room like he was a king and it his throne. He craned his head back toward the kitchen and smiled. "I'll still have room for apple crisp after this."

After everyone sat down with their plates, some in the small kitchen sitting at the table and the rest in the living room, Dario cleared his throat.

"Well guys, I have some really good news. I talked to the contractors at our new house today and they said they are finished." Everyone stopped eating for a moment. Drew was midway through chewing a meatball and he paused to hear what else his dad had to say. "With that being said, we can start moving our stuff in tomorrow."

The camper erupted in a cheer. Dario and Shelly caught themselves looking at each other from across the room and smiled. They had been cooped up in the camper, six of them, all summer and finally the time had come to move into their new house. After the initial bout of cheering from the kids, the camper grew quiet, the only sounds were them chewing.

Finally, Keegan spoke up. "I can't wait to see what it looks like now that it's done. I'm really going to miss this place though. This was the best summer ever."

"I agree, Keegan," said Jaime in her high-pitched voice. "We might have all wanted to rip each other's hair out at times, but this was my favorite summer too. Minus when Sodes left us for a while." She shot Sody a wink.

Drew finished chewing his meatball and he too spoke up. "I'm just glad I get to have my own room now. No more sleeping on this awful couch." He looked at his parents and smiled slyly. "Okay fine, I guess I had a pretty good summer too."

"How bout you, Sody?" asked Shelly, looking toward her son. "What did you think about this summer? It must have been pretty eventful for you between running away to Chester's and running away again around the lake. Hmm?"

Sody talked over a mouthful of wild rice. "Best summer yet, by far. In fact, I bet ten years from now I'll look back on these past three months and say the same thing. How can you beat a summer that showed you who you are?"

When he said it, he was thinking of the spirit of the north wind, but instead of being scared, he was thoughtful and reflective.

"So profound. A young Aristotle in the making," chuckled his dad.

Later that evening, Sody headed back down to the dock to watch the sunset. It was one of his favorite parts of summer, watching the sun sink and turn the sky beautiful golds and oranges and pinks and purples. There was perhaps nothing quite like a Minnesota sunset. Of that he was certain.

"There is a thief in our heads, Sody. In all of us."

Sody jumped from his seat on the dock. He didn't know his dad was standing on the shoreline watching the sunset as well. "And that thief is there to try to steal our dreams. Don't ever let it."

"Okay, Dad," he said as they enjoyed the spectacle of the painted sky. "I won't."

Sody already knew all about the thief. Had come face to face with it, in fact. He knew it could creep back unannounced on some cold, dreary day in November when the north winds start howling, but he wouldn't ever let it in. He had promises to keep. And miles to go before he could sleep.

Acknowledgements

I would like to express my gratitude to my wife, for her unwavering support and encouragement throughout the entire writing process. I am grateful to Dan King whose insights and guidance were invaluable to the early development of this story. I would also like to thank Alexi Lindquist for her revisions and improvements to the manuscript which helped bring this book to fruition. And to my Grandpa Frank, for showing me that no good story should go untold.

Made in USA - Kendallville, IN
17068_9798986298139
10.12.2023 1328